For my father,

Otha Charles Tidwell,

Who loved his family, friends, and life, and

Who loved to golf, even in the snow.

I love and miss you.

D1526660

Find my Author Page, Karen M. Tidwell, on Facebook

Cover Art and Design by Betibup22@gmail.com

Edit Critique by Owl Editing

The Boyfriend

First Edition

ISBN – 978-1520633336

To Abby,
Thank you so much
for coming to the
event! I hope you
enjoy it!
Karen M. Tidwell

THE BOYFRIEND

CHAPTER 1

A shadowy figure loomed over her as Madison shook her head, trying to focus her blurry vision. The blackness that had moments ago, overtaken her, crept away, and let light in once more. Her head spun, as did everything else around her. Squinting to see more clearly, she attempted to breathe in deeper, but hyperventilated and her heart rate sped up dramatically. Sweat ran down her back and face even though she felt a chill in the air.

"Get up. If you don't get up, I'll fuckin' kill you," a distorted voice spat as she laid in a crumpled heap.

She cringed at the bass in his voice and moved shakily to stand up. Tiny pinpricks of agony radiated from her hands. She looked down at them dizzily. They pressed against a hard, unforgiving dirt road where she had fallen.

That's right, I'm outside.

She winced and tried to push herself up. Her stomach swirled with fear. She choked back vomit that arose in her throat. Floundering in her attempt to comply with the fuzzy being before her, she fought to remember who it could be.

It struck her. Her friend, Tanya, had broken up with her boyfriend, Gavin, a day earlier. The girls decided to take a road trip to get away from the drama. The drama, instead, followed them.

Where is Tanya? Is she dead? What's going to happen to me?

It sounded as if his voice echoed from all different directions. His commands leapt from behind her and then were in front of her. The deep, boom of his voice continued to demand she move as he circled around her tauntingly. Gavin planted his feet and stood over her with his legs wide apart. The tips of his boots touched the edge of her hands. He ordered her to get up on her feet, as she inadvertently cowered at his. Gavin's well-muscled frame stood roughly a foot above her own height. Not an overly broad man, he still delivered the level of intimidation of someone twice his size.

As she got to her knees, Madison tried to shield her face with one arm as he bent over her and barked for her to hurry up. Her vision cleared and the brightness of the early September day struck her face. Her arm, which shielded more than just an unforeseen blow from Gavin, tamed the light of the sun. Madison squinted again, gathered all her strength, and stumbled to rise to her feet. She finally found her footing, but a sharp, vice-like grip pinched her elbow when he took hold of her.

Her other senses trickled back, along with her vision. She didn't know if she should throw up or grab her head in anguish. Her feet clumsily navigated the rocky road while he continued to pull her forward by the arm.

Something warm and wet ran down her forehead and cheek. It stung, but her whole body ached as well. Madison wiped at it with her free hand. With nervous anticipation, she brought her fingers back down in front of her face to inspect the liquid. She stared at the tips, now painted red with her own blood, then reached up again and found the open gash on her forehead. She touched the source of the small river of fluid. She fumbled, but quickly regained her balance. She couldn't remember how she had been cut, but she could only assume this must have been the cause of her nausea. She located the wound one more time, and her salty fingers licked the cut with a sting. She instinctively dropped her arm.

Madison's breath became arduous as she attempted to keep up with her captor and fear took a tighter hold of her. She looked past him in the distance and glimpsed her family cabin. When Madison ran to get help, she left Tanya behind. They made this arrangement together. Now Madison wished she hadn't, as she worried about what might have happened to her friend. In this moment, she knew she needed to keep calm and if she could, fight to survive.

Madison forced her gaze toward her attacker once more. As her eyes ran down the length of his body, it occurred to her she never liked Gavin. He had always filled her with a sense of dread whenever he looked at her. His wanton gazes unsettled her. A couple of times he had become visibly frustrated with her when she avoided his touch. It struck her as peculiar and inappropriate, but Tanya liked him a lot, so she kept her mouth shut.

Now in the woods, he turned toward her, seemingly to gauge their surroundings, but then his eyes fell on her. Unlike today, where many times before Gavin's tone of voice never matched his expression, she had no problem reading his face. He wore a smirk on his lips and his eyes laughed, however, it exposed something sinister behind them. Madison gasped inaudibly when they locked with hers and she wavered backward in terror. His grip only tightened to prevent her fall and once more, her need to throw up grew stronger.

At that moment, Madison smelled something strong and bitter. With caution, she looked down and saw the front of her light pink sweater stained with a yellowish, wet mess. The taste of vomit wasn't all in her head or her throat. Everything hit her senses at once, her memory, the light, the pain, the nausea, and the fear. She trembled.

A flicker of light flashed across her face. It jolted her from her thoughts, and she noticed the large blade of a knife glimmer in the sunlight. With one hand curled around the handle of the knife, the rough talon like fingers of his other hand grasped at her more tightly. Gavin pulled her towards her death.

She had begun to lose circulation in her arm and then he yanked on her again. She grimaced in pain. She tried to keep up with him, but she wanted to attempt another escape. She tormented herself briefly, wondering what that could mean for her friend's safety if she did. However, she still looked around to gain her bearings.

A twig snapped off in the tree line to the right of them. She felt his hold loosen as he turned his back to her to hear more clearly. He stopped and scanned the area, and listened with his head tilted toward the culprit.

Now or never.

Madison had to try to run again; even though her inappropriate wedged heels might trip her up, she knew she had to. They stopped at a point in the road where the trees arched over them and lent a refuge from the sun. Birds happily chirped and a faint breeze blew through the leaves on the trees with a soft rustled chorus.

In the moment when his grip slackened, she ripped her arm away as hard as she could and ran. She had taken one move forward into the escape when she felt her head whip back and the rest of her body followed. Sharp pain permeated her scalp where he held fast to her hair.

He whirled her around so roughly toward him, she slammed into his body. She struggled to pull them apart. His face only inches from hers, Gavin drew the knife between them and ran the blade along her long, bare neck. He spoke in a whisper and once again, his face mirrored the sound of his voice.

"Make me work harder for this and I will make you pay for it. I've got nothin' but time."

His hot breath silently blew over her skin and moved the tangled hair from her face. His lips pursed in anger. As quickly as it had appeared, a familiar glimmer in his eyes replaced the rage. He whistled as he grabbed her by the arm and resumed the journey back up the road.

Madison let Gavin tow her back toward the old cabin. The nostalgic home once filled with warm, happy memories had become awash with nightmares.

She never seemed to have a break from the waves of sickness that overcame her. Madison thought about what the odds were of a dangerous predator entering their lives. She quieted a laugh that threatened to emerge when she realized how slim it had to be. They apparently won some sick lottery.

She wondered if she should beg for her life. Too afraid to speak, she held her tongue and nervously waited for an opening he might give her, though he never did. The lack of words haunted her more than anything he had said that day. The rest of the trudge back to the small, log home came without so much as a grunt or a whisper. She only heard his strangely soft footsteps on the ground and she shivered.

As they approached the cabin, Madison faltered and tripped on the wooden porch step. As she lurched forward, it felt like he had ripped her arm out of the socket. He held to her firmly and never wavered. Where others might have gone down with her, Gavin seemed to be made of steel. She tumbled through the front door and sprawled onto the hardwood floor next to Tanya when he roughly released her. She hit her hands and knees so hard her teeth chattered and she groaned aloud.

Her friend's face went from shock to anguish when Madison fell beside her, but Tanya looked too terrified to speak. Tanya's right cheek and eye were red and puffy. The white of her eye itself had turned red from a ruptured blood vessel. Handcuffs linked Tanya's left wrist to the metal frame of the worn, green couch. The futon, where they once slept as children when Madison's parents brought them up for the weekends, now became their prison. She bit her lip to keep the tears back as she realized that up until that day she had taken her life for granted.

She crawled to rest beside Tanya, whose beautiful long blonde hair had become dirty and snarled. Open wide in fear, her one good eye watched her ex-boyfriend in terror. Madison noted that as he paced the cabin floor, he looked right through Tanya and focused on her instead. Still on all fours, she tried to rise to a seated position. Her battered friend reached out as far as the handcuffs allowed her, so she could help Madison. Finally, planted on her rear-end, they huddled close together.

Tanya whispered to Madison, "What's he gonna do to us? He's going to kill us, isn't he?" Tears streamed down her cheeks. Madison's eyes welled up with tears of her own and she wrapped her arms around Tanya.

Clasped fiercely to each other, Madison wracked her brain for a new plan. There had to be a way to get them out of this. They had to fight their way out. No other options presented themselves. With the two of them against him, they might stand a chance.

Madison leaned in toward Tanya, stroked her hair, and tried to whisper. No words escaped her lips before Gavin jerked her by the arm again, pulling her away from the comfort of her friend.

"Noooo! Please stop!" Tanya screamed in vain, as she tried to hold fast to Madison.

Gavin wrenched Madison free, and turned to face Tanya. He raised his index finger to his mouth, turned back to his work, and fastened Madison to the other end of the couch. He stayed in a crouched position in front of her as he spoke again for the first time since the driveway.

"Thoughts, Maddie? Something you'd like to share with the rest of the class? You sure are the trouble maker, aren't you?" He clicked his tongue and stared at her with such intensity she finally looked away. Gavin smiled, seemingly pleased with himself.

"I like a good challenge but I think it's time to end this game, don't you?"

"Wh..why…are you doing this? What d-do you want from-mm-ma us?" Madison whimpered.

"Whaddya mean why?" he bellowed into her face. The echo of his tirade shook the logs of the cabin. She shrank against the couch and wished she could disappear.

His voice now a heated whisper, "Why do you think? Too good for me? Tanya didn't think so, what makes you so fuckin' special?" In his squatted position, his knife dangled from his hands in between his knees. Gavin took in a deep breath and closed his eyes as he exhaled.

When he opened his eyes, his head cocked to the right with a sigh, and he examined Madison closer. Reaching out an open hand, he caressed her cheek and his face softened for the first time, but she shuddered reflexively, repulsed by his touch.

Gavin jumped up and roared one last time, "Fine, bitch! Have it your way."

He placed the knife back in the sheath and grabbed the cuff keys from his pocket. He unlocked Tanya. Her face full of confusion and alarm, she appealed for help with her eyes.

"What are you gonna do? Please I'll do anything you want, just please stop. I'm sorry, I swear, I didn't mean it." Madison blubbered as she begged for forgiveness.

"Too late," he said coldly. He grabbed Tanya by the hair

and dragged her across the floor into the back bedroom of the cabin while she kicked and screamed. Madison joined her friend's shrieks. She struggled with the cuffs as the door slammed shut behind them. Frantically, she scanned the room for anything that would help set her free.

The minutes ticked by, marked by the sound of a grandfather clock in the corner of the room. The tortured cries from Tanya went on for ten or fifteen minutes. Maybe more. Maybe less. She tried to reach the end table where she hoped to find a tool to crack open the cuffs. She stretched and contorted her body, but couldn't reach the table. She let go of the fight to catch her breath. As she sat there and tried to block out the sounds from the next room, she saw something shiny where Tanya had been chained. She stretched out her foot and pulled the object towards her. Leaning over, until her mouth found the silver chain, she picked it up with her teeth and released it into her confined hands. She recognized it as the necklace Gavin had bought Tanya. Blood from her fingers smeared across the inscription. She cried softly and let it drop from her hand back to the floor.

Madison's head whipped toward the back room when she heard what sounded like slaps and howls of misery. Her heart raced and she decided to give up the struggle to reach the table. Instead, she pulled on her own hand to wrench it free from its metal cage. Even if it cost her a hand, she didn't care. Flesh tore away from her wrist and the base of her thumb as she continued to wriggle and pull from the cuff. Her hand refused to budge. She pressed her feet against the legs of the couch for better leverage, as she heard the terror in Tanya's voice increase. The wails of torture intermittently interrupted by grunts and gags inspired Madison to push against the couch as hard as she could, one last time.

Frenzied, she pulled wildly, breathless while her heart pounded in terror, until a chilling quiet enveloped the quaint cabin. No more screams or grunts.

She looked at the handcuffs. Her blood and skin coated the bracelet, but freedom eluded her. As sweaty as she had become during her struggle, she still wasn't slick enough to slip free.

Behind her, a door hinge creaked, and her whole body froze. She forced herself to turn and look over her shoulder with her feet still planted on the couch. With as much bravery as she could muster, she looked up at Gavin, who stood inside the frame of the door. She could no longer hear or see Tanya. She turned away from him and heaved silent sobs, foreseeing her own demise.

Their day had begun so wonderfully. Tanya had regained her freedom and Madison had her friend back. They were set to go out to celebrate that very night, until Gavin had surprised them from the backseat of her car. *So close.*

CHAPTER 2

The already dark office grew dimmer with each minute that passed on the chilly fall night. A single light shone through the glass door of an interior office from a computer monitor, and bounced off Lauren's somber face. It stretched the shadows across the walls near the small desk she occupied. Dimly lit working quarters didn't appeal to most people, but she focused much better in this environment. Lauren's work ethic rivaled her skills with the keyboard as she typed in rapid surges to record everything the client relayed.

Every so often she would say things like, "ah ha", "yep", and "I see", into the headset that rested in her ear.

She bit her lip while she fought off the urge to yawn and forced herself to give the client her full attention. Lauren had learned in the last month, that by doing so she avoided quite a few headaches.

Her desk faced the wall, which meant her back faced the door. Many times, she would have preferred a different vantage point. Especially, on dark nights like this, when she knew that the building her employer resided in, had vacated all other tenants for the evening.

"Good night, Lauren." Lauren's chair toppled over as she leapt straight up. Her boss crossed in front of the glass window of her office. Her heart thudded loudly in her ears and she clutched at her chest to feign a heart attack before sticking out her tongue at Beth Brown, one of the names on the front door. The chubby middle-aged partner of Brown and Finch rolled her eyes and shooed her away with a wave. She scurried by, toward the exit. Once Beth left the lobby and Lauren's heart had slowed to a normal pace again, she swore she saw the shadows on the walls grow taller.

"Hello! Are you all right?" a voice nagged at her from the earpiece.

She returned to her chair, arched her back slightly, to straighten her posture, and cleared her throat.

"No, I'm still here. Sorry about that. I was startled by a co-worker," she apologized. Lauren brushed her long, straight, brown hair back with her fingers, and concentrated on the task in front of her. She continued to type as Sally Ackerman droned on.

"I gave him 12 years of wedded bliss and do you want to know what the piece of shit gave me? Nothing. And now this other woman -- half my age, unbelievable," Sally whined.

"Yes, I know. It really isn't fair," she agreed sympathetically. Lauren looked at her screen, which illuminated the room, and sighed in relief. She couldn't remember what Sally had said, but reflexively she had typed it.

Her long fingers paused on the keyboard and with her right hand, she grabbed the mouse to pull her email up. She clicked on the refresh icon and crossed mental fingers that a new email from her best friend would greet her with a happy hour invitation. When nothing appeared, she stared at it even harder, as if willing the message to materialize. The monitor seemed to glare back in refusal to bring her the good news she so desired. She rubbed her face with her free hand, unable to shake off the exhaustion that threatened to consume her. *I need to get out of here.*

She turned her attention back to Sally, who ranted about her husband's extracurricular activities. What should have been a breezy divorce case had turned into a nightmare. A month ago, Mrs. Ackerman had prided herself on the amicable nature of her breakup, which had elated Lauren. Her hopes since dashed when the Ackermans had become every other divorcing couple she had ever encountered; bitter, angry, and spiteful.

Lauren admitted to herself this could be a slight exaggeration, but the quick and easy cases were rare. Many times, over, she carried the weight of defeat on this career, but she needed the experience under her belt to move on. In addition, she adored her boss and the free parking.

Drained by the unbearable hours, counterfeit pleasantries with the clients, sob-filled phone calls from soon to be divorcees, and belligerent angry ones from the opposition, Lauren fantasized about long vacations or unemployment. She believed in her work, though she could now understand why a rumor surfaced about her Family Law professor. The rumor being, he drank frequently at a local bar and if his breath didn't confirm it for Lauren, working in the same field of law certainly did.

In class, he would talk about his clients and the horror stories. He would never name them, but rather he would give the horrible details of once happy couples that attempted to destroy each other, with their children along for the ride.

The other area of law she loved, didn't seem to fare any better. Her Criminal Justice professor also frequented the bar and had his own cheerful stories to share. He once told her, "Ninety percent of your clients are guilty, five percent are innocent, and five percent you just don't know."

Lauren always wondered what became of both of those professors after college. When it came time to pick which of the two she liked best, she decided to pick the lesser of the two evils. There in her dark little office she wondered about her choices as she continued to pick a fight with a computer about happy hour.

"I'm really sorry that Mr. Ackerman is dragging his feet, and I completely understand that you just want this over with and behind you. I really do. Let's just give it 'til next week and we'll revisit this issue with Beth next week," Lauren consoled.

As she tapped her pen on her desk, the hairs on the back of her neck stood up. She tried to focus on Sally's words, but rubbed her arms from the ice that passed through her body. Her eyes darted suspiciously around the room and she craned her neck to peer outside her office.

At the end of the main hall, past the small lobby, sat a large, lavishly decorated conference room. The partners of her firm wanted the clients to relax during a time burdened with stress. They had an immense fish tank built into one wall of the conference room and added a large floor to ceiling, wall-to-wall window, which looked out into the great expanse of the Twin Cities. At the right times of day, light streamed through the big window and into the calm waters of the tank, illuminating some of the brighter colored fish. It had also been known to hypnotize a child or two in the throes of a tantrum.

"Okay, great," she responded with hesitation in her voice. She relaxed once the chills had dissipated.

"Okay I just want to get this taken care of as soon as possible, I can't live like this anymore," Sally stated with exasperation.

"Well I'm sure we'll be in contact soon," Lauren promised.

"Okay, I really hope so. Thank you so much for listening to me vent, yet again. Have a great night, Lauren."

"Not a problem, at all. And thank you. You have a good night as well, Sally."

She hung up the phone, took a deep breath, shook her hands out at her sides, and cracked her neck. Leaning back in her chair, she clasped both hands behind her head and stretched as far back as she could.

"That's it. I'm not answering the phone anymore. I'm just gonna go home," she said aloud.

Most of the cases she had worked on, dealt with false accusations of all kinds, ranging from "simple" assault, to weird sexual requests from their partners, to horrendous violence perpetrated by the husband or the wife. Even worse were the true reports that put the false ones to shame.

Child custody cases were the most dismal. Instead of children's books on the coffee table, Brown & Finch should have child psychology books and an on-staff therapist for these poor lost souls.

"Enough of these thoughts," she said. Lauren could only hope Sally had someone else to confide in about her divorce.

Lauren stood up to collect her things and organize her desk for the next day, when the idea of a possible vacation entered her mind and a smile spread across her lips. Perhaps she would go to a quiet beach or a secluded resort, lay in the sun by a pool, and maybe enjoy some eye candy of the dark-haired male persuasion.

"Okay, after this case, I'm gonna do it," she whispered to herself. "Maybe I can drag Kelly along for the ride."

Kelly, her best friend was the only friend or family she had. Lauren never slowed down to make new friends and she no longer had any family left alive. She reached for the mouse to draft her own email to Kelly when she remembered she still had the headset in her ear. She eased the device back into its cradle. When the headset snapped into place, her computer dinged.

Her hand flew up, startled by the noise, and knocked the can of diet soda over, spilling it onto the floor.

"Shit!" She jumped out of her chair. Then her shoulders slumped upon seeing the mess she now had to clean up.

However, the new message box that had popped up on her monitor, brightened her office and her mood. *Talk about perfect timing.*

After she covered the puddle with a few leftover napkins from lunch, another ding echoed in the empty office.

"I'm coming. I'm coming. Sheesh." Lauren sat back down while her soda soaked into the towels, and clicked onto the icon. As she suspected, she saw Kelly's name immediately, and she opened the message with a grin.

I hope she wants to go out. Please. Please. Please.

"Oh Lord," Lauren rolled her eyes and giggled as she read Kelly's message about the new guy in her life.

Kelly had met him a few weeks prior at a party they had both attended. Based on her description in the bubbly rant she sent Lauren, this new guy's sweet and romantic nature swept her off her feet. Lauren had heard many things about Mr. Wonderful, a.k.a. Tony, from Kelly, but had not yet met him. Her hectic work schedule ruled her life and she had left before Tony bumped into Kelly that night. She had no real basis to make any judgments, good or bad.

Kelly and Lauren had long ago become accustomed to giving approval or disapproval of the men in each other's lives. Any new guy they would meet would be "the one" within the first few dates. However, their relationships didn't usually last long enough to warrant approval. They soon would be on the hunt for the next Mr. Right, so their opinions seemed moot in most cases.

Even with some of the creeps they encountered while dating, Kelly still managed to believe in love. For Lauren, the luster and mystery had faded away and she gave up her delusions, as she had come to think of them. The tantalizing pictures of hot exotic men satisfied her curiosity. She didn't want anything more than that in her life, not now, maybe not for a long while.

She had convinced herself that her career had taken up all her spare time, leaving her no room to date. The truth was, she could no longer emotionally deal with the chore of dating. The excitement of a new prospect would crumble when his true colors crept out, waving his freak flag high and proud

Alternatively, sometimes they simply disappeared. The only impact her career had on Lauren's relationships was the sour taste it left in her mouth.

Her fingertips had barely hit the keys in front of her to respond, when her phone rang.

After reading the caller ID on the phone screen, Lauren laughed as she picked up the receiver on her desk, "I just got the message. Would you give me a chance to reply?"

Her friend could never contain her excitement long enough to wait for an email back.

The two girls had been inseparable since they were practically in diapers. From break-ups to breakdowns and good news to even better news, they were always there for each other.

"I'm sorry, you know me. I've been waiting for the end of the day so I could bug you. So where did I leave off in the email? Did I mention what a great kisser he is? How wonderful he is? How nuts I am about him?" Kelly bubbled into the phone.

"Okay, okay. Slow down. You're hilarious and adorable. But seriously, it's only been a couple of weeks. Do you know how he feels about you?" Lauren asked, happy for her friend, but also cautious.

"Well it's been almost three, actually." Kelly corrected her defiantly but with giddiness in her voice. "And, oh, he loves me. Okay, maybe not loves, but he wants to spend every moment with me. Don't worry! I'm trying to follow the rules this time, so I have been putting him off from time to time. But, he's gonna love me. Who wouldn't?" She laughed.

The rules, Lauren sighed deeply at the reminder. Many books had been written on "the rules" of dating to safeguard its readers from a one-night stand and help them land a relationship. The authors covered all the key points, from when to accept the date, when to take the first phone call, when to allow the first kiss, and when to be intimate for the first time.

"I think I'm going to puke," Lauren teased sarcastically. "That does explain why you haven't been around nearly as much. It sounds like it's going really well with you two. And you're right, no man in his right mind wouldn't love you. Maybe in a month you could come up for air," she said with a grin.

"Yes, we are disgusting and we love it," Kelly snickered.

"Well, what are The Disgustingtons up to tonight?" Lauren fished, with hopeful anticipation.

"Dinner. Oh, I didn't tell you. It's so funny. I think he got a little jealous of my client tonight. He asked me if he was cute and single. Crap! He should be picking me up any minute though. I just wanted to brag one more time about how wonderful he is. Did I mention he isn't even pressuring me for sex after three weeks? How weird is that?"

The imaginary martini glass she held in her hand 'poofed' into smoke.

"It's truly a sad commentary on our world if three weeks of no sexual pressure is something to be amazed by, but the…" she trailed off when a flash of light reflected off her office window from behind her and caught her eye. She sat up and swung around.

"Yeah, isn't that the truth. How pathetic when we distrust every action of every guy we meet?" Kelly interjected with sarcasm of her own.

"Hey, I caught that." She half listened while she continued to search for the light from her seated position. She saw another glimmer of a light shine through the window that ran parallel to the front door. Her hair rose on the back of her neck for the second time that night. She watched intently for a few more seconds as Kelly spoke. A few minutes went by like this, with Lauren lacing the conversation with her typical work responses while she waited for another flash of light. Nothing.

Huh…

She shook her head as if she had been seeing things. Over the last few weeks, this very thing seemed to occur more and more often. Each time, Lauren felt a shiver of the creeps penetrate her flesh, or she would see something move out of the corner of her eye. Each time she would investigate, and each time it turned out to be nothing. She chalked it up to the late nights she had worked and the fatigue that came with those hours.

"I just know that you're trying to figure out if the jealous thing is good or bad. It was a joke, I'm sure of it." Kelly urged on the other end of the phone.

"Oh, well that's good. Oh wait. What?" Her back straightened ever so subtly when her friend's comment sunk in. "I hope it was a joke," she raised a single eyebrow, but Lauren knew she had a penchant toward the dramatic overreaction when it came to the men in her friend's life.

"Don't worry so much, Lauren. It was a tic-tac sized comment, no big deal," Kelly soothed. It wasn't a big secret Lauren tended to be a worrier, but after years of friendship it felt like Kelly could read her thoughts from time to time.

"Okay, well shoot. I wanted to meet for a happy hour. I hope you guys have a great dinner and we'll have to do drinks soon. I guess I'll wait for a call and you can share all the yucky gushy details later." Lauren overdramatized her voice to sound sad, but disappointment colored her mood.

"Hmm…that actually does sound good. Why don't you join us for a pre-dinner drink? I really want you to meet him anyway. You will like him, I promise." Kelly's voice hit new levels of squeal into the receiver, which Lauren believed must have gotten the attention of every canine in a one-mile radius.

"Yes. Oh good. I was hoping for a martini…I mean to meet Tony," Lauren teased, revitalized with the excitement of finally getting out of the office and her own home. "Where do I meet you two love birds?"

Lauren hung up after she wrote down the name of the restaurant, and subconsciously bit at a fingernail. Her tendency to worry had evolved into this new bad habit, which had replaced a cigarette habit, so she didn't mind the torn and nibbled nails as the price.

She understood people had jealous impulses, but it still bothered her for some reason. It appeared so soon in their budding relationship. Her paranoia could be interpreted as a good thing or a bad thing. Lauren had to fight her own instincts and keep her big unsubstantiated mouth shut. Intentions aside, her concern and protectiveness might be misread as negativity or jealousy when it came to a love-struck Kelly. Kelly wanted to think positively about each new mate and hold onto hope longer than she should, just as Lauren used to.

She donned her navy-blue suit jacket once more, covering her burnt orange, collared shirt. She hoped it wasn't too chilly out as she didn't bring a coat and her legs were bare under her matching navy pencil skirt. She unknitted her brow and shut down her computer.

Time to meet Mr. Right.

CHAPTER 3

On the short drive to the restaurant, Lauren hoped he truly would be Mr. Right, and not Mr. Questionable-at-Best. Kelly deserved happiness.

Timely as ever, Lauren arrived to the restaurant a half an hour late, but somehow, she still managed to beat Kelly and Tony, which struck her as odd. She disregarded any ill thoughts about Tony and forced herself to think only positive thoughts. Lauren imagined Kelly must have stopped off at home to touch up her hair and make-up. She had a habit of tardiness, even more than Lauren did.

She walked into the somewhat crowded, high-end restaurant with an uneasy knot in her stomach. Lauren entered the bar area and glanced around. There were high-top and low-top tables, as well as cozy booths, and to her relief, available seating at the bar. However, the main dining area drew in a crowd, making the lobby difficult to navigate. Patrons were strewn about either sitting or standing practically on top of one another, pagers in anxious hands. The atmosphere in the back appeared to be more dimly lit and intimate from what Lauren could see. The lucky customer's pager would go off and they would be led between two red curtains to their table. She pushed on to the almost full bar. They were one chair shy of accommodating herself, Kelly, and Tony. *I can always stand, if need be.*

When Lauren sat at one of the available high-top chairs, she placed her purse under the counter on a hook and signaled to the bartender for a menu. Lauren mentally calculated her bank account balance before she reviewed the drink list.

Well I can have three. Do I need three?

"I'll take a Cosmo." She folded up the menu and slid it back toward the bartender. As she sat there, she played on her phone and drummed her unpainted fingers on the bar top anxiously. The smooth and cold counter felt expensive and appeared to be made of black marble or granite.

As Lauren took the last sip of her first drink, she eyeballed Kelly who finally entered the restaurant. She choked on the cosmopolitan and set it down before she dropped it. The person that entered looked like Kelly, but she sported a new blonde hairdo. She tilted her head to the right and blinked repeatedly. She couldn't believe her eyes. She wondered if the light bounced off her hair in such a way that made her hair simply appear lighter. Her darker-complexioned friend normally wore jet-black hair. Kelly also displayed a fretful look on her face. Lauren realized her own mouth gaped open in shock, and she closed it before Kelly glanced her way. She tried to remain composed.

"Don't judge. This is your best friend and she has always wanted blonde hair, hasn't she?" she whispered to herself. She breathed in and out with slow purposeful breaths and tried to be "zen", or whatever people called it.

Not only did the new hair color and Kelly's expression trouble Lauren, but the man who walked in a close step behind Kelly, plagued her. He moved with an agitated, stiff, yet determined pace, and followed Kelly so closely his chin almost bumped the top of her head. It had to be Tony, though she wished for a coincidence. Perhaps a random stranger, irate about something else, happened to come up behind her when she arrived. That notion crumbled away as they approached Lauren together and Kelly introduced him.

"Hi," Kelly said rigidly. "Lauren, this is Tony."

Upon closer inspection, his body appeared tense, but he conveyed a calmness on his smooth and blank face. Kelly still wore the worry lines on her brow, but with a smile Lauren had seen many times before. The Public Relations smile, or PR smile as Lauren coined it. She knew it all too well and Kelly's eyes never lied. She used that grin to hide her anger, most times. This time she hid something else. Lauren tilted her head at Kelly with a question on her face, which made Kelly smile even brighter.

Hmmm. Okay then. Don't tell me. It's probably nothing. Just a silly fight. Should they be fighting already? No, Lauren. No negative thoughts. Do this for Kelly.

The two friends hugged briefly, then Kelly took a seat next to Lauren. Tony remained on his feet and stood behind Kelly.

"Hi Tony, I'm Lauren," She stuck out her hand to take his. The handshake, quick and firm, sent a shiver through her body. He gave her the creeps, but she clamped her mouth shut.

His hand felt slightly cooler to the touch than most, which reminded Lauren of the smooth, cold features of the bar. Internally, she laughed at herself. The weather had become increasingly cooler at night and they had just come from outside.

"Should we see if we can find another chair or a different place to sit?" Lauren offered since they were short a stool.

"Nah. Gotta stretch my legs. I sit all day for work." Tony bore a friendly enough smile, still something nagged at her. He definitely knew how to turn on the charm. From his entrance into the restaurant, through to the bar, his whole presence had shifted.

I'm not a paranoid person. Ok, now I'm lying to myself.

Lauren clapped her hands together and smiled at her new company.

"Well, I was about to order another drink so I could withstand the pitiful looks the bartender has been giving me. You know the ones you get from people when you have been stood up for a blind date," Lauren chuckled and spun around to grab the bartender's attention.

Before she could, he slid a fresh beverage in front of her. Perhaps he read the awkwardness between the parties and made a mental note to keep the booze flowing. She flashed a thank you smile his way and then he turned to focus on Kelly and Tony.

"What can I get you folks?"

"I'll have a brandy neat and she'll have white zin," Tony stated swiftly.

Lauren found herself curious about the interactions that took place between Kelly and Tony. Tony, full of questions for Lauren, seemed to take Kelly by surprise. Kelly's worried brow became a confused one, and eventually rested on a relaxed and happy expression after a few minutes. She laughed more comfortably, sipped her cocktail more freely, and leaned slightly into Tony. Her friend lit up and Lauren had never seen her like this. As Kelly played with her hair, she gazed up at him with twinkling eyes.

Lauren began to feel like she conducted an experiment. Tony and Kelly sat on one side of a mirrored wall, where they couldn't see Lauren, but she could see them. As she evaluated all their movements and words, she envisioned she ran a psychological study. The movie, <u>Ghostbusters</u>, sprang to mind. The scene where Egon analyzed a couple who thought they took part in a marriage counseling session, but in reality, he repeatedly turned the heat up in the room to document their reactions. She wondered if she should turn up the heat, so to speak. Though the thought had brought a smile to her lips, she knew doing so would cross a line with Kelly.

"Did I say something funny?" Tony asked directly.

Thrown off guard, Lauren's eyes widened and she shook her head.

"No, sorry, I...uh...I get distracted by thoughts from work a lot. It's not you. I get stuck in my head sometimes," she said chagrined.

Kelly nodded in agreement at her statement, "She does that a lot," she reassured him, but glared at Lauren, "It does get annoying sometimes."

"I'm really sorry. I truly am. It's been a long few weeks at the office,"

Something sparked in his eyes. Another brief shift in his demeanor and just as quickly, he shifted back to the charmer. She blinked a couple of times and from that point on she stopped thinking about 80s movie classics and gave Kelly and Tony her full attention.

He dove back into his barrage of questions and amped up the dazzle. Casual at first, he merely appeared interested, but if possible, too interested. After a while, the questions felt more pointed and personal. Even questions about their childhood together came up in the short time they sat there. Each answer Tony followed with a squeeze of Kelly's shoulder or a kiss on her head. He even winked at Kelly a couple of times when he told a joke. For Lauren, it felt deliberate or showy. *Oh, Lauren, cut it out.*

He seemed fascinated about how close the girls were and for how long. Lauren got lost in the conversation when college came up and forgot briefly to overanalyze Tony as they reminisced about the frat house.

At first, they simply told Tony stories about it, but soon they found themselves whisked away in the memory. Lauren could almost see the giant eagle statues, painted red. They functioned as columns on the porch, outside the three-level home. Nestled amongst other frat houses across from the college campus, the décor of these columns made it stand out from the rest. The old weathered eagles had been spray painted with yellow on their once proud chests with the fraternity letters, 'T K E'.

Practically, every weekend they would head up those old porch steps, through the entryway, and clamor their way inside to start the evening's festivities. The house would soon become dwarfed by the sheer number of young collegiate adults who attempted to get drunk and laid. One party had sprung to their minds and became one of Lauren's favorite memories of college. At least the parts she could remember.

Lauren and Kelly giggled when they realized how little they did recall, however, simultaneously they lost color in their faces as they regaled the events of the next day's hangovers. Lauren slept all day. Every so often, she dragged herself out of bed and crawled to the bathroom to drink water and throw up. Lauren's first and last mid-term she failed during her college years became another fallout of the night's hoopla.

Tony paid avid attention and hung on Lauren's every word. He looked down at Kelly and grinned. Lauren didn't notice until her story ended that his smile curled up like a villain's mustache in old cartoons. In her mind, she saw him rub his hands together and cackle while he tipped a black top hat.

"Did you have to hold her hair back all day or were you throwing up beside her?" he asked curiously.

They laughed together and then Kelly nudged Lauren when she added, "Lauren didn't come back to the dorm room. She puked in someone else's room."

His grin faltered.

"Stayed at another friend's place?" His tone had a faint edge of a growl with an emphasis on the word friend. It jolted Lauren for a moment. She returned to the conversation when she heard Kelly's snicker.

"Sure. Yeah. We'll go with "a friend", though I never saw him again after that," Lauren added with a chuckle, but her cheeks stained red. It wasn't her proudest moment, however, she immediately stuck her chin up slightly to defy any regret or shame.

Tony's eyes flashed and his smile completely faded. Lauren's back stiffened and she shifted in her chair uncomfortably. *That's weird, why is he upset about what I did?*

"So yeah, that was our wildest night in college, I think," Kelly broke the silence, "After that we graduated and began our career paths."

Whew, subject change.

Tony relaxed and slowly his creepy grin returned as did his questions. Next came questions about their families and before she knew it, it had been an hour. As she sat there and played with the napkin under her drink, it dawned on her she still didn't know anything about him. Since they had yet to request a table, Lauren knew she had some time to learn more about him.

She resumed her internal study. At roughly 6'2, average build, and reasonably attractive, he likely had a number of women from his past. His brown eyes matched the darkness of his hair, but his hair had a burgundy tint to it. It resembled the color on a home hair color kit she had seen before at a drug store. *Maybe he has greys?*

He had very strong, sharp features and full lips. Straight white teeth from expensive dental work, she suspected. He dressed almost militant. Nothing appeared to be out of place. No lint, no wrinkle, no crease, or anything. She figured he must be a neat freak who bordered on obsessive compulsive. He wore a grey polo sweater over a white collared dress shirt, paired with black, freshly pressed slacks. She didn't know men's shoes but they looked trendy and polished. *Tony, the brand new shiny penny.* However, she feared, he wasn't a penny, but simply cheap chocolate wrapped in copper colored foil. She briefly wondered what he did for work. She opened her mouth to ask when he lifted his wrist to look at his watch.

"Look at the time. Wow. It's getting late. If we want to eat anytime tonight, we better see about a table. And I just noticed a lull in the lobby over there, so this is probably the perfect chance to get in."

It sounded contrived and a convenient way to avoid inquiries about himself. However, he wasn't wrong. Even though the restaurant buzzed with chatter and the clink of silverware and dishes, the mob at the back of the restaurant had broken up. *Breathe. Stop. You are being overly paranoid and reading into everything*

"Okay, honey. Why don't you put our name in. I'll wait here with Lauren and catch up a little more," Kelly said as she reached up to give him a kiss on the cheek.

He pulled away awkwardly, at first, but quickly put his smile back on.

"Sounds good, but I don't think we will need to wait. See," he pointed, toward the recently emptied waiting area.

"Oh. Well I guess that's our cue," Kelly sighed.

Lauren tried to temper her own suspicions but the hairs on the back of her neck persisted and she shuddered. She inspected her own breath to see if it had become visible from the cold she felt. Nothing.

Kelly hugged Lauren good night. Her PR smile had faded away an hour ago, and had been replaced with a genuine one. Lauren curbed her concerns for now.

"Aieeee," Lauren yelped out in surprise when Tony grabbed her and gave her a hug after Kelly released her. Kelly laughed warmly, but Lauren, taken aback, felt uneasy. Even though he picked her up straight off the ground in a big bear hug, it felt cool, like his handshake. She then noticed his cologne. A potent stench. *I guess I'm washing this outfit tonight.*

He set her down, but not until she patted him on the back to indicate, he should. She waved goodbye to both of them as they headed off to the dining area.

She signaled to the bartender for her check, but he shook his head at her, "Mr. Anderson already paid."

Anderson?

She scratched her head.

The befuddled look on her face provoked him to explain further, "The guy that was just here with you."

"Oh sorry. It's my friend's new boyfriend. I didn't know his last name. Thank you," she said and attempted to tip him.

He only waved her off again, "He's covered everything. Thank you though," he nodded and rapped his knuckles on the bar before attending to another customer.

"Another 'nice guy' move," she said quietly to herself. With her wallet back in place, she picked up her large brown purse, slung it over her shoulder, and turned to leave. She stumbled backwards when she ran directly into Tony. When she realized what had just escaped her lips, Lauren wondered how long he had been behind her. Ashamed of her comment, she couldn't manage to look him directly in the eye.

"You scared me," she floundered.

"That was the point." He said it straight-faced, but the sound of forced laughter escaped his lips. "Nah, I'm just kidding, I am after all, a 'nice guy,'" he quoted her with his fingers. One side of his mouth curled up. She couldn't tell if the statement offended him or if he only teased her at this point. Goose flesh spread up her neck to her hairline and her stomach sank.

Apprehensively, she responded in an attempt to diffuse any ill will, "Yeah I didn't see that coming, you know, paying the tab. Thank you. It truly is a nice guy thing to do."

She patted him on the arm as a form of gratitude and an awkward move to distract him from the uncomfortable moment. He did not attempt to get out of her way. She pulled her arm back timidly when she finally made eye contact with him. She looked around him anxiously, but could see no way by him. He only

nodded in approval of her thank you, but his position remained
unchanged.

Lauren sensed something aggressive, almost predatory
about him and felt like his nervous prey. Her eyes darted around
the room in search for an escape route. She cleared her throat as a
final hint.

"Well, I should get going. Busy day at the office tomorrow.
You know, all those crazy divorcees." She gestured wildly with her
hands and almost hit him in the face. Her nerves sparked and
frayed at the edges.

Why won't he move?

"Oh of course," he moved fluidly to the left, but she still
had to step sideways and rub up against him to get past both him
and the barstool. She felt nauseous and she could feel his gaze
upon her.

"Tell Kelly I love her and I'm sure I'll see you again soon,"
she stammered, when she finally squeezed by him.

"Yep." He said.

With as much poise as she could muster, she tried to rush
out without giving the appearance of flight. She knew he still
watched. Instinctually, she hastened her steps when she breezed
through the glass doors and headed toward her car.

Once inside, she tried nonchalantly to lock the door. Lauren
had parked directly in front of the big glass window that
overlooked the bar. She could see clearly inside, which meant she

could be seen clearly too. Breath abated, she bore a trouble-free mask on her face as she stuck the key into the ignition. Lauren lifted her head when she threw the engine in reverse, and observed Tony walking back to the dining room, but with nothing in his hands. No drink. No food. No bill. No wallet that he stuffed back into his pants.

He had already paid the tab. Why did he come back? Maybe he just ordered a drink for delivery to the table. That doesn't make any sense. They would have a waiter. Stop being paranoid Lauren.

She leaned back, shifted the car back into park, and released the air she suffocated on.

"No, be paranoid, Lauren, "she muttered.

CHAPTER 4

Lauren walked through the door of her two-level townhome with defeat on her face. She dragged herself straight to the couch and dropped down face first. Screaming into the cushion until she ran out of air in her lungs, she then calmly, as if nothing had happened, pushed herself up. She smoothed out her black skirt and brushed back wild strands of hair from her face.

The Ackermans had dramatically increased the war they waged within the brief period of a week. Apparently, Mr. Ackerman's new and younger woman, now carried his child. Mrs. Ackerman tried to think of anything and everything to make him pay for his betrayal. Mr. Ackerman's attorney had threatened to file an Order of Protection because Mrs. Ackerman smacked him.

Lauren actually wondered why he hadn't filed one yet, but perhaps, Mr. Ackerman figured a simple slap in the face only equated to a slap on the wrist. Likely, Mr. Ackerman would want to sink his teeth in deeper, so he worked hard to sabotage Sally, and get her to snap in a big dramatic way.

Though Lauren sympathized, no matter how much Mr. Ackerman had changed, Sally hurt her own case with her antics. The job of her attorney became exceedingly difficult as they tried, in vain, to clean up after Sally.

Lauren sat in the dark of her little living room and looked around. A low shimmer of light over the sink reached out from the kitchen. She had yet to turn on any other lights. No pets, no husband, no family, just her and her little light in the kitchen. It made for a very quiet home this late at night.

As she sat there, absorbing the latest battle with someone else's loving relationship, she appreciated her quiet and uncomplicated life.

Lauren could come home and not squabble with or have to explain herself to anyone. She also didn't have to worry about what to do when things ended. There would be no division of furniture, pets, children, or bank account balances. No pain to be felt when someone moved on from her and found someone new to love. She could sit on her cozy sofa, turn on her big flat screen television, that hung above the fireplace mantel, and have complete control of the remote. She could prop up her feet on the coffee table; and maybe have a bowl of popcorn in her lap. Lauren didn't have to cook or argue about what to cook. She controlled everything in her home, which included her emotions. It seemed to her that whatever happiness people felt when the relationship began, it never lasted. She hated how much of a cynic she had become, but Lauren had yet to figure out how to shut it off. *Charming, I'm sure.*

A barking dog interrupted her thoughts. The neighbor dog often barked at leaves blowing down the street, but as she went to the kitchen window, she caught the glimpse of a light. It bounced in the dark, about a block away near the neighbor's house. He barked again. She stepped closer to the window. In the distance, she could see what appeared to be a small light move chaotically near some bushes. Every time the light moved, the dog barked. A shiver ran down her spine. Her breath fogged the window, making her aware of how close she now stood to it. She squinted but could no longer see the light, even as the frazzled dog began to yowl. Curious, she shut off the kitchen light to see if that would help her get a better look.

The hairs on the back of Lauren's neck tickled her. Goose flesh spread down her arms. She stared, unblinking, out the window for a few minutes. The dog fell silent, and the light didn't return. She closed her eyes and then opened them, looking one last time. Nothing. The tingly sensation faded, so she closed the blinds and turned the lights back on.

Lauren pulled off her mauve colored jacket, and draped it over the kitchen stool at the counter. She changed up in her room, throwing on a pair of leggings and an oversized sweatshirt.

Once back downstairs, she grabbed a glass from the cupboard and filled it with an already open bottle of Riesling from the fridge. She headed toward the couch once more, but thought twice and whirled back around to retrieve the bottle.

"Just in case," she said to herself.

Lauren carefully set the items from her hands onto the coffee table in front of her and sat down. Flipping on the television, she took a generous gulp of wine.

"Wow!" She looked at her glass, almost empty after the first swig, "I really *am* going to need the whole bottle."

Lauren gazed as the screen light flickered on. A news reporter's melancholy voice broke the silence of her home.

"...and after over a one-month search, the bodies, of 28 year-old Tanya Burk and 29 year-old Madison Talbert have been recovered. The autopsy is still underway but it appears they were both stabbed multiple times. The results of the autopsy won't be available for a few more weeks. While they have no suspects in custody, it does appear that the police do have a person of interest. Gavin--"

"No thank you! I have to hear enough bad news at my job," Lauren said aloud as she changed the channel. She didn't know what she should have expected from the news. She wanted to be on top of her current events and knew the news didn't always bring cheerful stories, but she just couldn't deal with more broken people at the end of a day like this.

"Bah! Who am I kidding? How much am I really involved in my community or the world around me? Most times, I just want to shut it out."

She took another sip.

"Man. I'm a downer. And I really need to stop talking to myself." Lauren twisted her lower lip in her fingers and contemplated going to bed, but chose to flip through channels instead. More thoughts tumbled into her head. She bit her lip as she struggled to keep the words in there.

Lauren landed on her favorite station and laughed at the irony when she realized how much she loved Law and Order, Special Victims Unit, but she couldn't seem to stomach the news.

Maybe I should watch a comedy instead of this dark depressing stuff.

She held fast to the stem of her wine glass when her body jerked in response to her cell phone that lit up and danced across the coffee table in vibration. Lauren grabbed it before it fell to the floor.

Great reflexes, if I do say so myself. Minor victory for the day.

Phone in hand, she glanced at her phone. Kelly's name and picture flashed on the small screen as it continued to shake in her hand. She swiped on the little green phone icon and took note of the time. 10:30 p.m. She hoped her friend hadn't been putting in similar hours as she had.

"Hey there. How's it going?" she said with a jovialness that surprised even her.

"Pretty irritated," Kelly answered annoyed.

"What's going on?" she asked. Lauren's brow furrowed and she realized she sat straight up on the couch. Kelly sounded angry, not frightened, so she couldn't figure out why she felt on edge and nervous.

Lauren did observe that when she thought of Kelly, she also thought of Tony. And when she thought of Tony, tiny brail like bumps jumped up on her arms and neck. She never mentioned to Kelly what happened at the bar, after she met up with them. Lauren feared the impact the conversation would have on their friendship. Even now, the mere statement Kelly made should not have had such an effect on Lauren, yet here she sat at the edge of her seat.

"It's not a big deal, Tony is just being ridiculous and I'm just frustrated and confused," Kelly vented.

"Okay, what happened?" She relaxed a bit.

In my defense, it is about Mr. Creepy.

"He's just acting all jealous and freaking out cause I worked late tonight. It's just bizarre. Accusing me of cheating and crap! Can you believe it?" Kelly sounded incredulous. "It's a long story that started last week after we talked about college. Can I come by? I really don't want to be here when he gets home."

Lauren thought of how moments ago she wanted to curl up in bed and pass out, but she didn't have to be up early. Bright side, the company would be a nice change of pace in this lonely house.

"Sure, I'll try to slow down on the wine until you get here," she feigned laughter.

"Okay, be right there with my own bottle."

Lauren disconnected the call, set the phone on the coffee table and fell back into the couch. She tried to catch up on the brief moment she missed on the show when she popped back up as something Kelly had said hit her over the head like an anvil.

What on earth did Kelly mean by not wanting to be there when he got home? Home? Home???

Now she stood on her feet, this time with a full glass in her hand. It seemed the wine magically appeared there because she didn't remember refilling it. She had begun to pace the living room and talk to the air.

"There is no way she'd let him move in. She would never do that after five or six weeks. It's ridiculous. Completely ridiculous. Maybe Kelly's been right all along and I'm just being paranoid. She probably is just letting him crash there or maybe I misheard her completely. I had to 've, had to…"

Speculation swirled in her mind for the entire twenty minutes it took Kelly to pull into Lauren's driveway.

Lauren peered through the beige blinds as she saw the headlights stream across the black pavement of her driveway. She replaced her wine with her nails. She removed them from her teeth and took one last deep breath.

Please let me be wrong. Don't jump to any conclusions.

She tried to open the white door that led to the living room with as little gusto as she could muster so as not to give away the frenzy she whipped up in her head. Lauren's attempt to stow the emotion on her face faltered, as she never mastered that skill. However, when the door flung open and Lauren's eyes settled on Kelly, all she could see were her tear-filled eyes that were red and swollen, and a botched attempt at a mascara repair job. Kelly thrust a bottle of white wine at Lauren and did her best to give Lauren the famous PR smile, but they both knew better.

The evidence of true hurt on her friend fizzled out the previous emotions that had coursed through Lauren's veins. Her desire to yell replaced with a desire to give her a hug and comfort her instead.

When they had finally sat down with a fresh beverage in hand, Lauren pressed for the details.

"Okay, what happened? Start from the beginning,"

Kelly took a sip of wine and regaled a more detailed version of the events leading up to their phone call.

"I had to work late, like I said. He just got angry right away and accused me of cheating. It's weird. Then he brought you up and that stupid college story. Asked if I ever pulled a stunt like that and called me a whore." She put her glass to her lips, but couldn't drink as the tears rolled down her cheeks again.

Shocked, Lauren couldn't comprehend what she had just heard and stumbled over words.

When they came to her, they flew out more harshly than she had anticipated or intended.

"What the hell? Are you joking? So you're breaking up with the jerk, right?"

To Lauren's dismay, Kelly's response that followed insinuated that Lauren overreacted. Kelly sniffled and took another drink before she set the glass down.

"It wasn't a huge deal, I'm just pissed. I mean I know it sounds bad and a... and I really wanted to break up, initially. He regretted it right away and tried to apologize. I just needed air," she stated matter of fact.

"Kelly, I'm serious. It is a huge deal. No guy should ever talk to you like that."

"I know, but it's just a fight, it's not like he hit me or anything. He just is a little insecure and worried that I will find someone else. His exes have cheated on him in the past. It's really not like him."

"Fine," She muttered. "You are an adult. I do have a question. Did I hear you right on the phone?" Once Lauren heard Kelly defend Tony's horrible behavior, she became inflamed once more and she couldn't resist another lecture.

"What did you mean on the phone when you said you wanted to be gone before he got home? Were you at his place?" She held her breath.

"No..." Kelly looked away before she finished her sentence. She avoided eye contact with Lauren. Lauren's stomach swirled.

"Technically, it's our place now," Kelly said sheepishly.

"I knew it. I didn't want to believe it, but I knew it." Lauren hopped to her feet. She regretted the tone as soon as she spoke, but she proceeded anyway. "Why on earth would you let him move in this quickly? You don't even know him."

"He had nowhere to go. He lost his place. I'm helping him out, if it doesn't work out, it's not like we're married. Relax." Kelly snapped as she folded her arms. Her face matched Lauren's in redness.

Lauren choked on a sarcastic snort, "I mean let's pretend the vulgar name calling is no big deal, but you can't live with someone you barely know. What are you thinking? And I can't help but to wonder why he lost his place?"

"Yes, I get it, but I'm just going to see how it goes. He does deserve a second chance. He knows I'm upset and he does feel bad. Don't get so worked up. I only wanted to vent. And not that it's any of your business, but he recently ended a relationship with someone he was living with. Would you want to keep living with an ex, especially if it was a bad break up?" Now on her feet, Kelly seethed in Lauren's direction.

Lauren's regret multiplied as Kelly's lips pursed while glowering in her direction. Her gaze shifted from Lauren to the door.

"I'm sorry, I didn't mean to get so…to yell, but the things that he's saying, they are all red flags. They are more than red flags. I just think you deserve better than that. No one should talk to you like that. I didn't mean to be so harsh," Lauren spoke softly this time.

Kelly's face untwisted, but her arms remained folded and she didn't make a move to sit down.

"Seriously, I'm sorry. I was out of line to yell like that."

The confident friend of hers looked so lost, beat down, and less and less like the girl Lauren knew. Dressed in her favorite maroon velour jog suit, Kelly had straightened her long wavy hair. She imagined that before the tears fell, Kelly's make-up had probably been applied to perfection. Kelly finally accepted the apology and took a seat on the couch. She sipped on her wine and looked at Lauren again.

"No, I understand," she exhaled. "I would feel the same way if it were you. Just trust me. It will be fine. It was only a fight, I'm not afraid of him or anything. I'm also not an idiot; you have to stop treating me like I am."

"I'm sorry; I don't think you are an idiot. I'm an overprotective nut, to a zealous degree," Lauren sighed. She didn't know what else to say. She couldn't convince her friend to do what she perceived to be the right thing. Lauren had to watch Kelly play this bad relationship out. A relationship they both knew wouldn't last and it frustrated Lauren to no end. Yet Kelly had to make this decision on her own.

"I won't say anything more. I know you wanted me to listen and that was all, so I will leave it at that. And you most certainly are not an idiot," Lauren stated again. Her friend wasn't an idiot, but she worried that perhaps Kelly had become love-blind.

The air, thick with awkwardness, needed to have some tension filtered out of the room. Lauren grabbed at a not so subtle subject change.

"So, what should we talk about next? Maybe the lax dress code at your office?" Lauren nudged her friend's arm as she joined her back on the couch.

Lauren couldn't help but to think, if Tony wasn't a threat of any kind, why couldn't she shake these goosebumps that continued to overcome her ever since they met Tony. She wanted to give her friend the benefit of the doubt. Yet again...

She rubbed her forehead and leaned back on the couch, but continued to wear a mask of happiness as her friend told her about her day at the office. It wasn't long before Kelly caught her not listening again.

"Lauren? Lauren? Hello? Are you even listening to me?" Kelly waved a hand in front of Lauren's face and giggled. "What were you daydreaming about now?"

"Sorry." She covered her mouth with her hand and grinned in genuine embarrassment, "I'm so sorry; it was a really long day."

After a lengthy pause, Kelly asked hesitantly, "Thinking about Tony?"

"Huh? Actually not at all, I'm serious, I'm gonna drop it."

"I don't mean like that," Kelly said with caution.

What on earth is Kelly talking about now? How much had I zoned out? How much have I had to drink?

She readjusted herself and rested her arm on the back of the dark blue couch, placing her chin in the palm of her hand. She just blinked at Kelly with an expectant look on her face.

"Well I wasn't going to say anything, cuz I know you better than that, but…" she drifted off uneasily.

"Buuuuutttt….whhaaattt…" Lauren made dramatic arms up in the air movements. Kelly fidgeted nervously and played with a loose thread on her sweatshirt.

What is she yammering about? This night is about to take another bizarre turn. I can feel it.

"Tony said that he came back to tip the bartender. You know, that night you guys met, and you were … you know... a little flirty. I just figured it was the drinks," Kelly teased and lightly pushed Lauren's shoulder.

"I mean, I can't blame you if you have a crush," she continued. "He is very good looking. However, I did tell him that you would never do that." On the surface, she defended Lauren, yet Kelly still stared at her quizzically and waited for an explanation or a response of some kind.

Lauren sucked in her breath and forced the air back out. The fact Kelly mentioned it at all proved she did not fully trust her.

What the fuck!?

Before she lost her mind, she tried to restrain herself. Lauren smooth out a lump in her sweatshirt, looked at Kelly's anxious face, and felt disappointed that someone who was practically her sister would even entertain the notion that she came onto her boyfriend. This was only made worse by the fact that Kelly seemed to have believed him, even if only a little bit. This was someone she had just met. Lauren found the words and spoke.

"Um no..." she shook from the level of anger ready to boil over. "I absolutely do not have a "crush" on him … at all." She made sure to act out the air quotes for her friend who had temporarily gone insane. The anger overrode any empathy she felt for Kelly and she didn't hide that fact well.

She went on, "Since you bring it up, I in no way would ever want to date him, let alone do I want you to date him. I can't for the life of me figure out why he would say that, but I can tell you this much, when I tried to pay, the bartender told me it was taken care of. And as far as the tip, the bartender also made it clear that Tony not only had tipped already, but had tipped well prior to you two leaving the bar.

Kelly looked confused, but not necessarily distrustful of her friend.

"Really?" She played with her hair nervously.

"Yes. I assumed I was being paranoid, but the whole returning to the bar thing struck me as odd. And he gave me a very bad, for lack of a better word, vibe. I was never going to mention it, but now this? Why the hell would he tell you I was flirting with him and then lie to you about why he went back to the bar?"

"Yeah, okay, that's weird," Kelly took a final sip of her wine and the smile had melted away. She pulled her blonde hair back into a bun and turned to Lauren, "Are you sure there was nothing he could have misconstrued as flirting?"

She sighed inside and shrugged her shoulders, "I was very uncomfortable. Maybe he read that as me being into him. You know men, right?" Lauren knew at that moment her friend had already made up her mind to forgive Tony, whether she believed Lauren or not.

Kelly relaxed her shoulders. Lauren had given her the excuse she sought. On the other hand, maybe, Lauren thought, Kelly feared she would have to choose between them and she wasn't ready to give up Tony.

"That has to be it, he just misread your weird, nervous behavior and thought you were flirting," Kelly said as if it reassured Lauren.

"Thanks a lot," she narrowed her eyes at Kelly. "If that was my flirting, well it would certainly explain why I'm still single."

"Likely does," she laughed. "He really isn't as horrible as I'm making him out to be tonight. I promise. You'll see. We need to have dinner together next time or a game night or something, so you can see who he really is."

Inside Lauren cringed at the thought, but hid it from her face.

"For you, I will give him another chance. Maybe next time it will be my turn to do the interrogation though," she said referencing his many questions.

They both giggled awkwardly and moved on from the topic. For an hour, they laughed and reminisced about their childhood together. They had lived a block away from each other in a small town up in northern Minnesota. They rode the same bus, practically had all the same classes together. They were "thick as thieves", except when they fought. They laughed about the one day where Kelly had been fed up with the pretty dresses Lauren's mom would make for her. As they fought in the middle of a park, one summer day, Kelly had noticed a pile of dog poop by the swings. She took advantage and shoved Lauren and her new pink dress into it. Lauren had no other recourse except the threat of no snacks at her house. As they reminded each other of these moments in time, they laughed so hard they wiped away tears. They almost forgot about the reason she came to Lauren's in the first place, until Kelly's cell phone dinged an hour later.

Instantly, Kelly tensed and Lauren bit her lip in agitation.

Lauren sat forward and put down her empty glass. Aggravation took root again as she realized this lovely evening drew to an end with a simple text from a guy whose freak flag had begun to flap in the breeze.

Kelly put her phone in her purse after she responded back with a message of her own. She rose from the couch with her glass in hand.

"I can pour you another if you want?" Lauren offered hopeful she could entice her to stay.

"No thanks. I should be on my way, big day tomorrow. And Tony wants to talk. I'm sure he wants to apologize in person; and I think I should let him."

Lauren knew a lie when she heard it, especially when that PR smile returned on Kelly's lips.

CHAPTER 5

"So, we have nothing?" Joshua fumed. He took one large hand and raked it through his short peppered brown locks. The other hand slammed down the receiver of his phone into the cradle. He wore a wrinkled, blue, two-piece suit and there appeared to be a few days' worth of stubble on his strong jaw. He pursed his lips so tightly they turned white and the pressure created a slash where a set of fuller lips normally resided. As he sat, rankled, at his old tattered desk, he grabbed eye drops out of his top drawer to rid his green eyes of the blood shot. The frustrated detective didn't know how many more dead-ends he would be able to stomach in this case.

Detective Joshua King took female victims personally. Moreover, the anger radiating from his body seemed to burn through everyone in the Minneapolis precinct. A familiar voice broke through the tension.

"King, we're still processing the last of the evidence, but it isn't much. Unfortunately, there aren't any witnesses," Joshua's partner, Gus, stated. "And as far as the lake where the girls were found, well we just don't have any new leads. This guy's clean, good, or just lucky."

Joshua looked in Gus' direction, who breezed past a rookie officer headed towards him. He promptly dodged him, but not before almost being knocked over by the young cop. He had bolted away from Joshua's bellowing.

"Hanson...watch where you're going," Gus scolded gently.

When Gus got close enough to Joshua, he leaned in and whispered, "I think you scared the new guy."

Joshua looked around his partner toward a young, but largely built officer with dark hair and pale skin. Officer Hanson seemed shriveled, but Joshua simply rolled his eyes at the newbie's fear of him and looked back down at his paperwork.

Happily, the scared pup had scurried back to his desk where he took calls on the tip line, his face still red with humiliation. Joshua heard Gus choke on a laugh. If he weren't so wrapped up in this case, he might have felt a twinge of guilt for causing Hanson's embarrassment.

Joshua King had a bark worse than his bite, especially when it came to newbies. Even though Joshua had five years of age and experience on him, he knew Gus had more wisdom and patience. However, Joshua's fire drove him to a higher than usual success rate in case closures. They were the perfect partnership despite their differences.

Unlike Joshua, the stocky Gus did not entertain the single life. He married his high school sweetheart, Miranda, after college. The polar opposite nature in the two men further highlighted their physical appearance. Gus sported blond hair and blue eyes on a pale, chubby face.

Joshua, the cliché detective, dedicated himself to his job. He would go on the random date here and there that Gus tried to set him up on, but nothing usually came of it. No one held his fascination like his job.

His face twisted even more in the general direction of Gus, who only snorted back at him. He knew Gus wasn't to blame, but he had very little sleep since he caught this case. From the moment the two girls had disappeared, it grabbed his attention, and it seemed to have enthralled everyone else in the station, as well. When they were found dead, he demanded the case from his Lieutenant.

The medical examiner put their times of death at about three weeks prior to when their bodies were fished out of the lake. Even worse, the water washed away most of the evidence.

In their file, a mysterious boyfriend of Tanya's no one had met, except for the other victim, came up several times in family interviews. Besides the name of Gavin, these relatives had nothing else to give the exhausted detectives. They also had a phone number for a disposable cell phone. That quickly became a dead end. This Gavin person appeared to be a figment of Tanya's imagination.

Who knows? Maybe she did make him up. Maybe she was some pathetic girl who couldn't get a date, or one of those girls that lied all the time. There's no way to prove he's real.

Joshua's thoughts ran wild. He wondered if they were going in the wrong direction, but he quickly dismissed the thought when he had to remind himself, Madison had mentioned Gavin to mutual friends too. Back to Gavin as his number one suspect. One he couldn't locate.

Looking up at Gus, Joshua responded, "I know, Gus, but who is this guy? How can he possibly be this invisible in these girls' lives? No one's ever met him? Where did he work? Where did he live? Nothing? He has to be brilliant! A fucking genius!" He stood up about to unleash another rant, but leaned back on the top of his desk.

Gus, who struggled to keep his own eyes open, turned to grab a cup of coffee. They both put in their fair share of long hours lately.

Joshua didn't expect an answer anyway.

"You want one?" Gus said as he poured his. Joshua barely acknowledged him, just shook his head, but stood up and followed

Gus, so he could continue to bluster. Gus stirred in about six packets of sugar.

"Or maybe it is someone completely different and this Gavin person is floating in a lake somewhere too. Which if that is the case we have to start…"

"Detective King. Detective King. Line 1…I think we have something" a red-headed officer interrupted him from across the room. The entire precinct seemed to hold their breath as she transferred the phone call to his desk.

He almost tripped when he turned too quickly to pick up the phone.

"This is Detective Joshua King, can I help you?" he breathed hard into the speaker.

"Yes this is Jen. Jennifer Collins. Madison Talbert's cousin."

"Okay…" he grabbed a pen off his desk and scribbled her name into a note pad. He tore it off and quickly shoved it at his partner. As Joshua continued his conversation, Gus rushed to his computer to verify the identity of the caller.

They had so many good Samaritans with false tips and crazy people with bad tips. They had family and friends who called constantly for a progress report. They even had a few psychics who also called in, or people who claimed to be a relative to one of the slain women and turned out to be just another crazy person. The hundreds of calls and emails they received turned out to be useless. The families of both girls got together and offered a reward for any information, which caused the call volume to go up astronomically. This only managed to increase the difficulty to find any good leads. They wasted hundreds of man hours that week just to go through them all. Sadly, they had to go through each and every single one. They couldn't risk the one good lead slipping through the cracks.

"Well I'm at the family cabin right now in Brainerd. This might sound odd, but it's clean..." she trailed off with doubt in her voice. She must have heard how ridiculous she sounded, Joshua thought. He sighed silently and kneaded his face as if he scrubbed away the sleep deprivation.

"Family cabin? Brainerd?" He rolled his eyes and chalked it up to another dead-end. Even if Joshua believed her story of being Madison's cousin, she probably had become paranoid or wanted nothing to turn into something because she felt helpless

Another misdirection or false lead.

"Yah. It's something Madison never used. I mean, she used to go all the time with her family, but never by herself. She was afraid to be here alone at night. No one's been out here since she went missing. We wanted to help look for her and then … well…when she was found, we, uh, just decided to forego the rest of the season and shut down the cabin. It wouldn't be the same without her." She sniffled into the receiver. Joshua could hear her take in a deep breath before she spoke again.

"I went up to lock it down now that winter is on its way and it's cleaner than I have ever seen it. I just thought it was strange."

After a pause, Joshua could hear her sigh.

"I guess I'm being stupid and probably wasting your time. But I asked around and no one's been up here since Madison... I don't know, maybe someone cleaned it before. Maybe I'm grasping at straws..." she said nothing more, but she didn't hang up.

Joshua jerked his head up when he heard Gus snap his fingers one desk away and gave him the thumbs up on Jen's identity. Joshua leaned forward, slightly more interested.

Well at least she is who she says she is. That's a start.

"Is there anything else? Any reason to believe that they would have gone up there?"

"Not that I can think of, but … I …uh I just wanted to be sure that I did everything in my power to help. It seemed off, so I thought I'd try."

"I completely understand, Miss Collins. We can definitely check it out. If it's nothing, I'll let you know. What's that address again?" He wrote with renewed fervor on his notepad.

"Can you stay up there until we get there? I'm gonna call a local police officer and have 'em secure the area. It's gonna take me and my partner a few hours. And one more question…"

He stopped and hesitated, afraid of her answer. If this turned out to be their only lead, he hoped for the best.

"Uh, have you touched anything, moved anything around? Did you start doing anything before you noticed anything suspicious?"

"No, not at all. I'm outside on my phone. I don't get reception in the cabin." She put his mind at ease.

"Good, stay there and don't touch anything. It may be best to wait in your car. Try to retrace your exact steps back to the car if you can. Thank you again, Jennifer."

Joshua couldn't take any chances on the preservation of evidence though it could be construed as slightly overboard to have her retrace her footsteps. If it turned out to be the scene of the murders, a lot of evidence would have been lost already and mostly because of the passage of time. If it was Mother Nature versus Jennifer's few steps back to her car, Mother Nature would have done the most damage he guessed.

He hung up the phone and glanced up at his expectant partner. He didn't know why he had a change of heart on the idea of a clean cabin being enough of a reason to look, but he felt a bubble of excitement. Not to mention, he couldn't pass up the only real tip they had since the bodies of these two women were found.

Half of Joshua's face turned up in a grin before he asked Gus, "Road trip?"

Gus's only response was a nod of his head as he grabbed the car keys, and shoved a notepad in his breast pocket. He stretched out his arm for Joshua to lead the way. He seemed to have lost the exhaustion in his face and Joshua noticed he didn't even bring his coffee. Perhaps Gus felt as rejuvenated by this bit of news as he did.

He said a silent prayer that this would lead to something and break this case, so he could finally get some rest. Joshua always submerged himself in his cases, which Gus would tell him made him one of the best cops he knew, but it wore on him.

Joshua had a younger sister. She would have been about the age of the two victims, if she were still alive. Renee had died at the hands of her boyfriend. Once Joshua received the information of a mysterious boyfriend of Tanya's, he went into overdrive on the case. Joshua couldn't help but to picture his sister in the crime scene photos; mentally transposing her face over the faces of Tanya and Madison.

Granted, he knew Renee's killer. Renee never filed reports of abuse and they had no evidence that linked her boyfriend, Chad, to it. Filled with shame and fear, like most domestic abuse victims, Renee also protected her secret as well as Chad from her older brother and the rest of the police. Chad made it look like an accident, but her friends had told Joshua of the frequent bruises that would come and go. They repeated the flimsy excuses Renee made up whenever they asked her about them. Then they told him of the threats she issued regarding their friendships if they made a big deal out of nothing. Eventually, they stopped bringing it up at all.

Unfortunately, it wasn't enough to indict, it wasn't evidence, just stories. Chad Stanton walked. Ever since this incident four years ago, any case that even smelled the same, Joshua worked with tireless determination. He wanted to punish all the Chad Stantons in the world. Maybe if enough of these guys were punished, Joshua would feel Renee finally got justice somehow.

However, Joshua knew deep down, it would never be enough. Not until he somehow got Stanton. Sometimes he scared himself when he thought about wrapping his hands around Chad's throat and squeezing until life slowly left his body.

His sister hid this horrible life from him and he blamed himself. In his mind, he should have seen the signs, but he didn't. He held a very successful arrest and conviction record, but the few times he couldn't make a charge stick, it would take weeks before he would climb out of the dark hole he sulked and hid in. As Joshua approached the driver's side of the car, he bumped into Gus.

"I got this," he reached his hand out to Gus to take the keys.

"Man, you're tired and it's a long drive. Take a nap."

"We're both exhausted and quite honestly, I feel good right now," he stuck his hand out again.

"When is the last time you slept?" Gus didn't turn the keys over, just gave Joshua a sideways glance.

"Just give me the keys," Joshua grew impatient with Gus.

Gus threw his head up again and mouthed a prayer.

"I'm tired, not blind. Seriously?" He glared as he grabbed the keys from him and got in the driver's seat. Gus shook his head and went around to the other side of the dark blue impala.

As he buckled his seat belt, Gus got on his phone to the Brainerd police headquarters to request an officer to secure the location, and to make them aware they were on their way. If this place turned out to be the scene of the murders, they would still be able to continue their investigation without conflict in regards to jurisdiction. Hopefully, these two city detectives could collaborate with the local investigators.

"This is going to be a damn long drive, maybe we can go over the evidence again. Have it fresh in our minds. You know for when we check this place out?" Joshua suggested.

"So, no nap for either of us," Gus instantly put up his hands in front of him when Joshua threw him a sour look. "I was just asking."

"You know me. I don't take breaks."

"No, no you don't," he chortled.

Joshua had the entire file memorized and even most of the crap tips they received. Gus retrieved his notepad out of his pocket anyways and shrugged his shoulders in acquiescence.

"I don't want to forget anything that we might need to keep our eyes peeled for," Joshua elaborated.

As Joshua slowly pulled out onto the freeway and focused on the road, he addressed Gus again, "Okay, so what do we have so far?"

"Two women, ages twenty-eight and twenty-nine. Best friends for roughly ten years. Tanya, the 28 year-old, dated a guy named Gavin, that no one besides the other victim, Madison, had ever met. Madison, twenty-nine years old, single, and didn't have any problems with anyone. Not that any of her friends or family reported, anyway. She worked at 3M as a secretary for a VP. Tanya worked at a cell phone company as a customer service rep. She also didn't have any enemies to note. Only link to mystery boyfriend is a disposable and apparently untraceable cell phone. Dead-end there," Gus paused as he flipped through his notepad for the next bit of information. Joshua grew impatient in the thirty seconds Gus took to gather his thoughts and interjected with his own list from memory.

"The truck was backed up to the lake from a launch, far enough to dump the bodies and not leave any foot prints. Tire tracks, but from every vehicle that ever used that launch, and long gone by the time we found the girls. And the abandoned truck was registered to Tanya Peterson. Another dead-end. No foot prints. No surveillance. Madison reportedly felt like she had been followed in the month leading up to the murders. The only description they could tell us was non-descript at best. Light brown hair, brown eyes, average height, average build. Way too many suspects in our suspect pool. Especially because they met online. Oh I almost forgot, one giggly friend did mention that Tanya gushed about how cute he was."

"That is some description, think we can use it? APB on an average guy, that's really cute?" Gus interrupted with a stupid smirk on his ruddy face.

Joshua rolled his eyes at his friend's attempt at humor, "Moving right along…"

Gus shifted in his seat and cleared his throat. Now it was Josh's turn to smile when his friend got the message and continued reading.

"Murder weapon, appears to be a knife, nothing solid from the coroner yet, and probably a knife the killer still has on him. And since we have no foot prints at our original scene, let's hope this is our murder scene. And let's hope he left something behind," Gus finished.

They both sat in silence, wanting the next piece of the puzzle to be useful somehow, but they already knew that unless this cabin panned out, they still had nothing. Going over the evidence repeatedly wasn't adding any new evidence or changing their current situation.

Joshua squirmed in his seat and rested one arm on the center console. With his left hand on the wheel, he briefly glanced away from the road to look at Gus.

"Let's pray this cabin is the end of the dead-ends."

CHAPTER 6

Lauren watched from a distance as Beth Brown shook hands with a tiny, frail-looking woman. She appeared to shrink away from Beth's outstretched hand, and her eyes constantly flitted around the room. Lauren could tell by the way that the woman wrapped her arms around her own body and her jittery behavior, that she was the victim of abuse. She tried not to stare, but couldn't help it. Her eyes continued to drift back toward them as she observed the pair by Beth's office. Her heart ached as she watched this woman, draped in baggy clothes with sunglasses in hand jump nervously at every noise around her. Lauren couldn't see any bruises from this side of her, but it had been an overcast morning—those sunglasses weren't meant to block out sunlight.

Finally, the woman confirmed Lauren's suspicions when she looked right at her. Lauren caught a glimpse of the purple discoloration around the potential client's eye. She wondered if she could feel Lauren's gaze on her. Lauren immediately broke the eye contact and moved papers around her desk as if she had been busy. From time to time she ran her finger along a calendar that hung on her window to give the impression she had not gaped at her.

After a few minutes, the woman still stared in Lauren's direction. It didn't take much longer for Lauren to realize the woman wasn't looking at her at all. She had zoned out in her own thoughts, much like Lauren did every so often.

Phew! Perhaps she hadn't seen me rudely gawking at her.

The woman turned back to Beth and nodded absently at something she had said. Lauren finally tore her gaze away from the direction of the poor woman and Beth. She sighed deeply before she faced her desk, now satisfied of her curiosity. She shook her head and grabbed a new case folder to open.

She set the folder on her desk to await Beth's instructions and pulled forms from a file cabinet that she knew they would need. As she put items together, she thought about the upcoming game night this evening with Kelly and Tony.

She drummed her fingers on her desk as she contemplated whether she should cancel.

Kelly would be pissed on one hand, but on the other hand I wouldn't have to spend any more time with Mr. Creepy. I just need to buck up and deal with it. Or, get it over with.

She packed a simple trivia game in the trunk of her car as her contribution to the night. She brought it deliberately with the hopes that any knowledge he had of any particular subject might answer more questions about himself than he seemed to answer willingly.

After a few more drums of her nails on the desk, with her chin in the other hand, she grabbed her mouse to open her email. As she clicked on the tab, a pop up box flashed open at the same moment. A new message blinked at her and she chuckled.

Wow, Kelly and I are definitely on the same page lately.

However, when she clicked OK, she didn't recognize the email address that appeared.

Junk mail?

The blank subject line peaked her interest and Lauren's nosiness won out. She clicked on the view option, so the message didn't open all the way, in case it was a virus of some kind.

No links were contained within the message either, only one simple sentence in all caps.

WATCH YOUR BACK

She stared for some time before she realized she had a death grip on the mouse and her heart raced uncontrollably. She let air in once more and tried to be reasonable. Clearly, she didn't recognize the address from where it originated. She figured it had to be a mistake or some strange spam message.

She hoped she hadn't left the company open to a hacker, but deep down she preferred that to a veiled threat.

Phwap! The pile of paperwork smacked on her desk in mid thought. The surprise caused her to whirl around so fast in her chair she had to grab onto her desk to keep from toppling out of it. *She has to stop doing that to me!* Lauren looked up at Beth, and she could see the distress in her normally cheery face. Strained with worry, empathy, and what looked like helplessness, Beth didn't even notice the near accident Lauren almost had. Taken aback by the emotion on Beth's face, she forgot about making fun of herself. Her boss never backed down to anyone, let alone showed fear or defeat. Even when she lost in court, she never gave opposing counsel the satisfaction of seeing that on her face. She guessed this attitude probably transcended into every facet of her boss' life and she respected and admired that.

Whatever this new client told her must have cracked that exterior. Beth leaned against the doorframe to Lauren's office and folded her arms and tilted her head upwards trying to hide the audible sniffle. When she finally brought her head back down to look at Lauren, Lauren could have sworn she saw water in her eyes.

"This is a pretty bad case, as I'm sure you saw on Tracy Mason's... The woman with the shiner is Tracy Mason, by the way. Anyway, it's a fucking shit storm," Beth quickly looked around to be sure there were no clients left in the lobby.

She looked relieved when she realized she hadn't just cursed in front of any.

"I did notice her and her shiner." Lauren frowned.

Beth continued, "Unfortunately, it's just the tip of the iceberg. I can't stomach to repeat what she told me. Just know that after two hours of conversation, it's the worst damn case I've ever taken. All my notes are in the file, so at least you get to read it instead of looking into the eyes of this poor woman while she gives vivid details." Beth stared off into the distance. She wore the same faraway look she saw on Mrs. Mason's face not ten minutes before.

"Beth?" Lauren reached out and touched her arm. Beth looked back at Lauren and smiled.

"Sorry, it's just … Anyway, for tonight, just scan through it. Don't ruin your night with it, save that for Monday."

Lauren just looked at her, not sure what else to say.

"Just be aware. It's the worst case I've ever seen or heard and I don't even know if we should be taking this case to be honest, but I tend to be dumb. So here we are."

Lauren picked up the stack of papers and watched her boss walk back to her office silently. She looked down at the first page of Beth's notes and several words caught her eye right away. Scribbled here and there across yellow legal notebook pages were rape, torture, contusions, and other words she didn't want to look at.

He seemed happy and excited when he abused her?

Not completely unusual, but this guy was sicker than most.

How was he not in jail?

Without reading the file in its entirety, Lauren knew this case would be a nightmare that her boss promised. It would even challenge the Ackerman's in a blood sport and win. This woman suffered, and the man she married appeared to be a dangerous sociopath. She wondered if she and Beth should consider hiring a temporary security officer, at least until this case settled. She bit her lip and researched the new client's soon-to-be ex-husband with the help of the internet. To know the level of danger this man posed could only aid them in their decision with security. At least it could aid Lauren's argument for one, if necessary. At the same time, Lauren would also dig into Tracy's background. They would need to know about any skeletons she possibly had before they went to court.

It didn't take long for Lauren to determine with the numerous police reports on file that Mrs. Mason wasn't inventing anything, but what if she held back information that was important for the case. Lauren learned to be as thorough as possible in the last few years, even with things that she didn't need to research.

As she pulled up her search engine to look up Mr. Mason's past transgressions, Kelly crossed her mind once more. She typed Tony's name into the search engine since she at least had a last name now, common, or not. He proved to be nothing more than a ghost. No Facebook, no Instagram, or twitter. Lots of Tony Anderson's would pop up, but none of them appeared to be him. She should have been relieved she didn't find anything, but it didn't sit well with her when she found nothing at all. *Not even a parking ticket?*

She would have preferred to find something prior to game night, so she could show up prepared.

Lauren continued to write some things down on a notepad in her searches for Mr. Mason, as well as, print some items out. She was about to fill out some requests from the police department when Beth came back into her office still despondent.

"Hey, you know, it's Friday. Why don't you just pack up and take an early weekend?" she leaned against her wall again.

"Are you okay? Do you need me to get you anything?" Lauren offered.

"No, I'll be fine. I definitely need the weekend after this and next week is not going to be fun for either of us, so let's enjoy our time while we can," She cracked a smile, but her eyes reflected her sadness.

"Okay, I'll shut down and head out. Have a good weekend, Beth. Maybe have a couple of drinks or shots," Lauren laughed weakly.

Excited for a few hours off work early, she quickly packed up her desk and grabbed her phone. As she headed out of the office and toward the elevator, she pulled up Kelly's number.

Maybe we can get started early and have some alone time.

"Hello?" Kelly breathed into the phone.

"Hey there. Guess who got out of work early for the first time in months? Me. That's right. I thought maybe I could come there now, and we can have some girl time until Tony gets there?" Lauren said happily.

"Oh yeah, that would be great. I'm still cleaning up for the game night though, so I hope you don't mind."

"Not at all. I should be there in about thirty minutes." Lauren said goodbye and ended the call as she exited the elevator on the ground floor. She walked towards the front doors down a long empty hallway. In this small quiet building, many people closed up shop early on Fridays, especially in the fall when the kids went back to school.

When she was twenty feet from the doors, a familiar tickle at the back of her neck struck her, and she had the desire to stop. She looked behind her. Nothing. She looked to all directions. Nothing. She took a slow step forward and glanced out the double glass doors that led to the parking lot. A blur ran past the doors. She faltered and took a step back.

That was weird.

In a fearful stupor, she gripped the wall next to her. When she saw nothing more, she took another brave step forward. Nothing. Another. She heard an engine revving. Once again, she stopped afraid, but something took over her body and she ran for the doors.

A gold four-door mid-sized car squealed out of the parking lot. It was already gone before she got a look at the driver. All she caught was the color, but no figure behind the wheel and no plate.

It could be nothing. But why did the hairs on the back of my neck go up?

She rushed to her vehicle. When she approached, she grabbed at the handle. Simultaneously, she realized she hadn't unlocked the car, but it released easily under the pull of her grip and popped open.

Huh? Maybe I didn't lock it? Or maybe I unlocked it and just don't remember?

She looked into her car and didn't see anything out of place. She climbed into the driver seat. Once all her items were in the passenger seat and her seatbelt buckled, she turned over the engine with ease.

Well no one messed with it anyway. I must have forgotten to lock it.

She pulled away and drove on to Kelly's house in dire need of a drink and girl talk.

A few blocks from Kelly's her phone rang in her car. She pressed the icon when she saw Kelly's name scroll across the digital screen on the radio.

"Do you need me to stop and get anything?" She guessed.

"No, but Tony apparently got done with job hunting early, so he should be here any minute. I guess we all get more time together. I hope that's okay," Kelly told Lauren hesitantly.

Her shoulders drooped instantly.

"No. Yeah, that's totally fine," she lied.

"Great. Well we will see you when you get here. Oh, before I forget, can you park on the street so Tony can park in the garage?"

"Absolutely, unless he beats me there."

They ended their call for the second time that day and with a sense of self-doubt, she proceeded onto Kelly's house.

She edged up next to the curb on Kelly's street in front of her white rambler. Just in case she had beat Tony to the house. She also noticed that Kelly's vehicle was on the street too, which struck her as odd.

Wait a minute, Kelly always parks in the garage. Why did she give her up spot?

She grabbed her bag of games and snacks out of the trunk with less bounce in her step. She trudged up the side walk to the front door.

When Kelly knocked, the door flung open and she knew immediately that she had not beat Tony home. *Home...ugh...*

Overly happy, he appeared to try too hard with his Cheshire cat grin that greeted her. She had no way to prepare her reaction in time and couldn't hide the immediate disdain when she realized it wasn't Kelly. Any happiness Lauren had in the previous moments on the walk up, had melted away from her face. She cursed herself internally when she could see Tony register her disapproval. His right eye twitched in response before his cheery disposition returned.

"Come on in Lauren. We've both been very excited to see you," he oozed.

"Oh, thank you," she stumbled over her words as Tony immediately pulled her jacket off.

She gave Kelly a hug who stood right on the other side of the front door. Kelly finally broke the hug, but Lauren clung to her.

"Sorry, I just miss you," Lauren stammered. Kelly giggled at her friend's weird behavior and pulled her into the kitchen.

"Should we start the festivities a little early? I made us cocktails."

"Yes, please." Lauren practically tore the glass out of Kelly's hand and didn't even ask her what it was.

Lauren fidgeted in her dress clothes as she eyed up Kelly's comfortable sweats with envy. Now a night that she presumed would be uncomfortable became noticeably more so, as she became aware of her stiff business attire.

Kelly made delicious appetizers, or perhaps she bought them, as she wasn't known for cooking skills. This was a fact that Lauren constantly teased her about.

She chewed on a stuffed mushroom and took a seat at the kitchen table.

"Rum?" she asked as she took another sip.

"But, of course. Tony says he has the next drink. He knows a top-secret, mouth-watering recipe. So, he says," Kelly bumped her hip against him.

"Really? What's the big secret?" Lauren said looking up at him.

"Well if I told you that it wouldn't be a secret. It's a family recipe, but I'm sure you will love it," he smirked.

"Okay, but I can't really mix my liquors, I don't wanna get sick."

"Don't worry." He said nothing more, just moved to a chair across from her. Kelly sat next to him and she touched the top of a game box.

"Trivial pursuit?"

"An oldie, but a goodie. You know how I suck at this game…so cheating is unnecessary, Kelly," Lauren said pointedly.

They both laughed, but Tony remained oddly quiet.

Kelly set up the game in a silent kitchen.

"Oh, I didn't tell you about the weird thing that happened right before I got here," Lauren piped up in an effort to alleviate the awkwardness that suddenly took place.

"What's that?" Kelly perked up.

Lauren proceeded to tell them about the strange figure, in a black hoodie, at her office and the email.

"I assume it was nothing, but it was super creepy."

"That is creepy. And the crazy message, I don't know. Maybe you should talk to your boss, Lauren." Kelly said with genuine concern, but Tony remained silent.

"I'm sure the message was just junk mail and the hoodie guy was just a coincidence and I'm certifiably insane," she said as she threw a piece of popcorn at Kelly.

"Or maybe the guy wasn't there for you, a little arrogant thinking it's about you," Tony finally spoke, and the hairs rose on her neck in response.

Kelly and Lauren sat silent for ten seconds before he laughed.

"I'm teasing, sheesh ladies. No, Kelly, is right, perhaps you should consider talking to your boss, if it happens again," he added. Though he let loose a hearty guffaw, his eyes remained cold and unaffected. Lauren tried to stop her body from a reactionary shudder.

Try for Kelly. Try for Kelly.

"Yeah, you guys are probably right. How about this? You two kick my ass at this game. After I try a famous beverage from your man, that is." She feigned a smile as she tapped her now empty glass.

One game went rapidly and like the first time she met Tony, he seemed to dodge any questions Lauren had for him. He did answer the general, non-personal questions, like where he had previously worked and how old he was and what attracted him to Kelly.

After her second drink, Lauren excused herself to the bathroom.

"Man, I'm already feeling the drinks after just two," she chuckled at herself in the mirror. She washed her hands, examined her make-up, and decided it wasn't smeary yet from the booze. As she dried her hands, something in the mirror caught her eye. Behind her in the closet, a black cloth stuck out between the doors. She opened the closet to shove it back in.

She didn't know when she began to hold her breath, but the air finally whooshed out as she pulled the crumpled black hoodie out of the closet.

"It has to be a coincidence," she whispered voice cracked.

Why hide it in a bathroom closet? Fearful, she tried to rumple it exactly the way she found it and left some of the material sticking out. If he was the guy from work, she knew it wouldn't be wise for him to know what she had discovered.

Besides, black hoodies, everyone has those.

She rejoined the duo who were in the middle of a passionate kiss.

"Eh hem," she cleared her throat loudly while looking at the ceiling.

"Sorry," Kelly giggled as she removed herself from Tony's lap and sat back in her own chair.

"No, it's fine. I totally get it. Just a little awkward for me," she teased. Lauren's heart rate returned to normal and her face relaxed. The exchange between the couple made Lauren second-guess her find and what she thought it meant.

She calmly took her seat and popped another mushroom in her mouth while Tony gently pushed a refilled glass toward her.

"Oh, thank you. I could use that after my miserable loss."

He wore a boastful smirk, but the alcohol made her less aware of those pesky flags.

CHAPTER 7

"Is this the turn?" Raising his hand to block the sun from his eyes, Gus squinted at the directions. He glanced back up at the sign, as Joshua slowed down.

"Guess so. God, I hope we got something here." Gus nervously clutched the address in his hand and stared out the window as they approached the small cabin. A cloud of dust rolled behind them on the way up the driveway, a small dirt road they traveled on. Parked at the end of the driveway sat a black and white police car. The middle-aged officer in the squad stepped out of his vehicle to greet them. Joshua and Gus pulled up next to him and flashed their badges.

"Your witness is over there," the officer nodded in the direction of the red Buick, where Jennifer, Madison's cousin waited with an eager look on her face. Joshua nodded back and put the car in park next to hers.

He wiped his damp hands on his pants, shocked that he was sweating from the anticipation. The belief they would find something of value and the fear it would be another stalemate messed with his heart rate. He wondered if this was the same for Jennifer, excited that she might have helped or terrified that she had wasted their time.

Confusion spread across her face as she continued to look back down the road past Joshua and Gus. He followed her gaze and saw nothing. Then he looked back at her dubiously.

"Where is everyone else? Are you guys it?" she finally asked.

It clicked in Joshua's head what she meant and it explained the confused look on her face. Jennifer expected the Calvary. The huge variety of crime shows that aired nightly on television easily threw the viewers off to the true nature of a criminal investigation. The mundane parts, such as the time to get labs back, search warrants, paperwork, and on and on. He leaned toward the open window and shook his head before he explained.

"No, not yet, Ms. Collins. First, we need to be sure that this is, in fact, the crime scene. If Gus and I find something, we will get forensics up here right away, but not until then," he informed her. A crushed look crossed her face and Joshua passed a sympathetic one her way.

"I just wanted to help catch her killer if I could," she clenched the wheel of her car. "I hope I did. Helped I mean."

He set his hand on her forearm that rested on the window of the car door. He felt like a broken record, repeating the same canned phrase to every victim's family.

"This is a big break for us. This is very helpful, Jennifer. I am truly sorry for your loss and I will do everything I can to find her killer." Rehearsed or not, Joshua meant it every time.

Preoccupied, she simply nodded at his gesture. The wind blew through her long brown hair as she took one last look around. Jennifer brushed her hair out of her face and finally turned back to Joshua, "Am I able to head out? I don't want to get in the way."

"Yeah, you're good to go. Why don't you head home, I'll contact you if we need anything else, or find something," he promised her.

"Thank you so much. I would really appreciate it. If you need anything from me I can pop over anytime," she handed him a business card and drove off.

He watched her drive back down the long driveway until she disappeared past the line of trees. He squeezed his eyes shut and wished he would find something, anything that would give Jennifer, and the rest of Madison and Tanya's family, closure. The violent nature of the murders was bad enough, but the killer seemed to have put them through torture. The bodies talked, but without the crime scene, the picture remained incomplete. Nothing but unanswered questions. He rubbed his three-day stubble and glanced around. The radio of the patrol officer's car crackled through the quiet of the wooded area. It went off every so often with back and forth chatter. Nothing serious that they could hear. The rustle of leaves in the background from animals that moved around or just the wind, sounded above them in the trees. Birds and squirrels chirped and chattered at each other near the cabin.

This isolated little shelter out in the middle of dense trees and foliage provided the perfect location for a murder. Joshua felt confident no one would have heard these girls scream, if they screamed. He desperately wanted this to be the place and he wanted a big fat sign that showed him the way. They had a long way to go, unless the killer stood in front of them with a tattoo on his forehead that read, "I DID IT". The bodies were found a couple hundred miles away from here. He needed a link before he could get the force out there, and unfortunately, the manpower is what he needed to help him find that link a lot quicker. *Double edged sword.* The more and more time that slipped away, the less likely they were going to find this guy. He sighed and took a step toward the cottage.

A surge of excited anticipation coursed through him with the first step closer to the cabin. An electric current seemed to surround him and pulsed stronger with each step. He knew in his gut something would be found within these wooden log walls and exhaustion slipped away completely.

"I'll start with the outer perimeter and see if I find anything. Then I'll come join you inside," Gus said as he went around to the back.

Joshua only nodded, vaguely aware Gus had spoken to him. He felt a force pulling him inside and the rest of the world seemed to fall away, except for the direct path up the porch, through the screen door, and finally past the creaky wooden front door. Joshua expected dust to fly up or at least see it float through the air where the sunlight spilled in through the opening. Nothing. Joshua doubted some vagrant wandered through here, crashed for a night, and as a token of appreciation, cleaned up after himself. Jennifer's presumption seemed to be correct. Joshua depended on the fact that statistically every criminal, no matter how meticulous, will miss some piece of evidence. They will leave some trace of themselves behind. He just had to be more thorough than the killer. Joshua rested one hand on his hip and the other on the holster of his gun as he scanned the room in contemplation.

He closed his eyes, putting himself in the killer's shoes. If he had been here, where would the best place be to hold them captive? He moved over to the couch and bent down to examine what appeared to be scuffmarks. He reached into his coat and pulled on his latex gloves. Lightly, he traced his thumb to feel the scratches left in the metal. He turned his head to the right to look at the other leg of the couch and found similar marks, but not as deep. The deepest grooves he found were on the back of the left leg. The metal bar that ran from one leg to the other would be an ideal place for chaining someone.

But wouldn't you be able to move this thing?

He pulled on the couch to judge how easy it was to lift. He managed to move it, but not easily. In fact, it had quite a bit of weight to it. Madison and Tanya weighed less than this couch by at least half if not more. He looked at the kitchen sink that held plastic containers in them, with no faucets. No running water, which would mean a lot more work to clean this place up. Joshua glanced down at the large blue plastic tubs next to the sink. Water jugs. Joshua made a mental note to have these tubs swabbed for evidence. He picked up a jug that was half-full and examined the lip, but couldn't see anything out of the ordinary, although he had been hoping to see what looked like dried blood. He wiped his brow with his forearm and set the jug back where he found it.

He opened the cupboards and examined the exterior and the interior. He felt under the edges of the counters and scanned the one bedroom cabin with his eyes, looking for something suspicious before going over everything inch by square inch.

"Yo King!" Gus bellowed from the backyard as Joshua bent down to look under the sink. He jumped up, smacking the top of his head on the counter.

"Shit," he mumbled as he rubbed his head. He glanced around the room, his pride wounded even though no one was in the room with him.

"King, I got something," Gus yelled again.

"Just a minute! I'll be right out," he responded. Joshua bent back down to pick up the pen he had dropped during his altercation with the countertop. As he stood back up, he noticed the rug slightly puckered in the center, directly in front of the couch. For some reason, the need to look beneath it overwhelmed him. His skin prickled with goose flesh, as his hand neared the corner of the carpet, and only became worse as he pulled it back. Time stood still as he hoped to reveal what could only be a treasure beneath. *Could it be?* Cut into the wooden floorboard was a perfect square and in the middle of that square, laid a flat handle.

He began to sweat again with giddy excitement. From a brief glance, he could see this area had also been wiped clean. He desperately needed the crime scene people to test for blood. Somewhere inside, he knew that this door contained the answers he sought. As a precaution, he drew his weapon before grabbing onto the handle and pulling it up. One last deep inhale of breath as he revealed the secret hiding spot, but loudly exhaled as he stared blankly at a layer of black dirt. He holstered his gun and grabbed his flashlight to get a better look at the small storage area. Joshua figured the space could only be about a foot deep, so he wouldn't be able to maneuver his body into this hole. With care, he scanned the ground with his flashlight. He heard the screen porch swing open, and knew Gus had lost patience with him and came to get him.

Joshua didn't turn around as he stated, "Sorry I thought I found something." He got down on his stomach to see how far this storage ran. He looked to the right and left. Nothing. Disappointment overcame him in a giant wave.

"Oh well," he added, discouragement lacing his voice. "It sounds like you found something though," he said into the hole. He switched sides and peered toward the front door under the floorboards. As he pulled the flashlight back out, something glimmered in the beam as it passed over it. He scanned back over the same area as slowly as his hand would move. His wrist shook, but he saw something twinkle in the darkness about two feet away from him under the hardwood floor. Could be nothing. Likely a penny, a nail, some sparkly bit of junk that had somehow fallen between the cracks of the floor before the rug had been purchased. However, the excitement he had tried to stamp out boiled to the surface once more.

"Can I tell you what I found? I mean, if you're interested at all?" Gus snorted behind Joshua, as he squirmed around on his belly. Joshua heard Gus sigh with exasperation, but it only mildly registered. He wanted to get ahold of that shiny object. Joshua sat up to scan the walls and the ceiling. Very quickly he focused on the skylight above the kitchen. Once again, his eyes skimmed across the room as he got up quickly.

"Can you tell me what you are doing at least?" Gus said with his right hand clamped around his notebook.

"Sorry, there is something underneath the floorboards and I need something to reach it. Aha. Found it," Joshua exclaimed. He spotted and grabbed a long metal rod that rested behind a broom and a mop, but was longer than both.

"What is that?" Gus asked as he stared at the strange long pole with a hook on the end.

"It's to open the skylight window, and it may be long enough to reach whatever is under there," he stated. Too focused on his main objective, he had yet to make eye contact with his frustrated partner. Joshua flopped back down on his stomach, faced the front door, and angled the pole back under the cottage floor. Gus rolled his eyes, grabbed his flashlight, and got on the floor next to Joshua.

"Where do I point this thing?" he said as he tried to be Joshua's eyes. Joshua stopped awkwardly balancing his own flashlight with the hook, and set it down.

"About two feet up and slightly to the right. It will shine when you hit it with the light," Joshua instructed.

Gus scanned for about ten seconds before he finally hit the object that lit up from the small shine of the flashlight, and Joshua immediately reached for it with the pole. His shoulders strained as he repeatedly stretched for it through the dirt. Each time he retrieved nothing but air. He feared this frantic clawing would only manage to bury whatever he saw, and they would need to dig up the floorboards anyway. He sighed and for the fifth time he extended out to grab his prize once more. Pulling it towards him, he and Gus could see what now appeared to be silver coming closer and closer to them. He picked the pole up and tossed it to the side, stuck his hand beneath the floorboard, and excitedly grabbed a fistful of dirt along with what appeared to be a heart shaped locket on a chain. Sifting through the dirt, he traced the locket gently and with both hands carefully opened the locket. Only one picture stared back at him. Tanya. The other side of the locket remained empty except for a small dot of dried glue. *Bastard took the photo.* He turned the heart shape ornament over in his hand and read the inscription that appeared to have dried blood on the back of it. *Forever and Always.* He wondered how it got down there.

He got up and headed toward where the locket had been hiding. Joshua could see that there was a wide enough gap at this point in the floor for the necklace to fall through, if it had come off Tanya. *Perhaps one of the girls deliberately threw it down here?* He couldn't know for sure. But he could see scuff marks leading from the bedroom to the edge of the rug.

It wouldn't nail a conviction, but enough to call the Calvary that Jennifer desperately waited for earlier. They could search the rest of the house.

Joshua looked at Gus with a huge grin, "What did you need to show me now?"

Gus rolled his eyes to the ceiling, and just gestured for Joshua to follow him to the back of the cabin.

"Surely your little find is enough to get forensics down here, but nothing wrong with a little added something, right?" Gus huffed sarcastically, as they headed around the house.

"Absolutely, the more evidence the better."

Joshua finally stopped ogling his prized locket and looked up.

"Nice find, partner," Joshua said as he approached a bloodstained tree. "Do you think we'll get lucky and the bastard left some of his own blood in here?"

"Not likely, but based on the notes from the M.E., she had pulled imbedded bark and wood particles from the contusion on Madison's forehead. And from what I can gather, the mark on the tree seems to match her height. At a glance, anyways." Gus already had a Q-tip with a blood sample in a plastic baggy of his own, but more samples would be collected once the crime scene unit arrived.

Joshua had desperately whispered a prayer once more. This time he prayed that the killer had also left a trace of himself somewhere in all the foliage. He knew he shouldn't get too greedy, but he couldn't help the deep desire to finally put this case to rest and give these families peace.

As thoroughly as the killer had cleaned the rest of the cabin, Joshua breathed a sigh of relief they had discovered anything at all, let alone the two things they had found. Bewildered that the killer had failed to notice this, Joshua found himself locked in a mental battle in his own head.

Perhaps he didn't care that her blood was outside in the middle of nature. Perhaps he thought Mother Nature would do her thing and there wouldn't be anything to find in a few days, weeks, months. Perhaps he wasn't that worried about the girls being identified, but then why clean up the cabin? Was he giving himself time, was it OCD?

"Yo! King? Can you perhaps let me in on your thinking?" Gus snapped his fingers in front of Joshua's eyes.

He pushed Gus' hand away.

"Yes, I'm just confused. Why clean up, but miss or ignore these things. Okay, the necklace, it was hidden, but this? I'm just trying to wrap my head around why he would take the time to clean up the cabin and dump their bodies elsewhere, if he was just gonna leave this?"

"Very good questions. Maybe he simply didn't care if the girls were identified. I mean he may not have planned for anyone to notice something like a clean place," Gus sighed and began to head toward the car.

"Where are you going?" Joshua ran after him.

"There isn't much more we can do here. Forensics will be over this entire place now that we have something solid, or something at all. They are more equipped. We did our job, now we get to rest, right? The local PD will wait for the forensics team to get here. It's all good," Gus patted Joshua on the shoulder and stuck his hand out for the car keys. This time Joshua knew Gus wouldn't take no for an answer.

CHAPTER 8

"Nooooo!" Her muffled voice tumbled over her fat and numb tongue.

Lauren grappled with a heavy sensation of semi-paralysis, as the awareness of hands on her face, in her hair, and on her body, gave way to an immense desire to flee. The air felt thick and her movements were slow and clumsy.

A shadow hovered over her, but she couldn't focus on it.

Am I dreaming? Am I drunk? What's going on?

Her eyes kept closing as she fought to keep them open, trying to cling to consciousness.

Where am I? Kelly. Where's Kelly.

Her arms went up again and futilely hit a face with no force, then slid back down to her side.

Lauren's eyes were open now. Everything blurred and ran into one another, like a painting. She attempted to reach up and rub her eyes, but her limbs failed her repeatedly.

"Tsk tsk tsk," a deep contorted voice said as her eyes shut again.

I have to be dreaming.

The brightness of the room assaulted her. She blinked her eyes slowly. Luckily, the cloudy vision slightly protected them.

Oh man! Am I hungover? I didn't even drink that much.

She stretched slowly and laid still, afraid her head would explode if she sat up. After a few minutes, she realized that besides being tired and slow, she had no other symptoms of a hangover. She closed her eyes and tried hard to remember what happened last night.

After a couple of minutes, she relaxed her body, though frustration burned through her. She couldn't remember anything, other than becoming extremely groggy during the middle of a game the night before. *Did we even finish the game? I remember mushrooms and drinks…and the hoodie!*

Her eyes flipped open and scanned the room when she heard someone moving around.

"Good morning, Lauren. Boy, you and Kelly cannot hold your liquor," he chuckled.

Tony. She opened her mouth to reply, but felt nauseated. Something itched at the back of her brain. A tremble ran through her body and she reached for the blanket that was draped over the back of the couch, pulling it over herself. Though fully clothed, she felt exposed and vulnerable.

"Good morning. What time is it?" She refocused on the ceiling. She felt violated somehow, yet nothing seemed out of place. However, she couldn't shake this vile sense of being touched somehow. It stuck to her skin and the intense yearning to shower screamed inside of her.

"It's still early, I'm about to make breakfast if you're interested." He appeared in her line of vision and lingered above her.

Okay, I gotta get out of here. Where's Kelly?

"Oh man. Thank you but, I have so much to do." She forced the words out while she awkwardly sat up, still clutching the blanket close to her chest. Like the remnants from a nightmare, a queasiness stuck to her.

"Well that's too bad. I was gonna whip up some bacon and eggs. Kel's in the kitchen having some coffee."

Lauren begrudgingly craned her neck to look at him and wished she hadn't. He wore a new expression on his face she hadn't seen before. Arrogance, knowledge, contempt, or something else.

"Hmmm…maybe a quick cup with Kelly." *Anything to get*

out of this room with him.

Lauren rushed past him and helped herself to a cup before seating herself at the table next to Kelly. The only sounds that came from Kelly were groans and grunts here and there. She was about to ask her incoherent friend how much she had to drink when Tony glided into the kitchen and stood in the door.

"Are you sure you don't need anything?" his voice reverberated in her head and the creepy sensation intensified.

Lauren just shook her head and tried to give a friendly smile. She choked and spit out a mouthful of coffee when Tony sent a slimy wink in her direction.

"Hey, Kelly," Lauren whispered while patting her friend on the head. "I gotta get home. Lots of cleaning to do this weekend. Once in a lifetime opportunity with no work."

Half-asleep at the table, Kelly just nodded and gave another grunt. Lauren kissed her on the top of the head and narrowly slid past Tony, who crowded the door.

As she stepped outside, she called out to Kelly, "I'll be in touch soon, love ya."

She shuddered and shook as she walked towards her car, but then she paused in the middle of the driveway. A thought struck her when she saw Kelly's car on the street, and remembered the parking arrangements from last night. She looked back toward the house and couldn't see Tony in any of the windows. Her bravery or stupidity took over. Fixated on the small one car garage, like a tractor beam from some sci-fi movie, it pulled her toward it.

What do I even expect to find anyway? She may just be that boy crazy and gave her parking spot to this jerk willingly.

Yet she couldn't stop moving her feet forward. The seed had been planted in her head, and it could not be dug out, no matter how stupid the seed. Until she could peek through the window and assure herself that the black hoodie was mere coincidence, she wouldn't stop for anything. Almost anything.

"Hey." A bark came from behind her.

She let out a scream and whirled around. Him again.

"Oh God…um…you startled me," she said breathlessly.

"You forgot your jacket." He stared at her curiously. "What are you doing?"

"Oh..I..uh.. nothing. It's really stupid. I thought I heard a noise in the garage, but it must be this hangover messing with me." An insecure laugh bubbled out.

Before he could ask her more questions, she grabbed her jacket from his outstretched hand and rushed towards her car.

"Thanks again." She waved and hopped in.

CHAPTER 9

Lauren took a big gulp of her soda and stared at her monitor. The white light illuminated her little office as it had many nights before it. And like those other nights, everyone had gone home for the night, long before she put together the final touches on the Order for Protection for Mrs. Mason. Apparently, she didn't already have one. This seemed to be a common theme with her clients lately.

She lightly chewed on the cap of her pen and looked at the clock on the right-hand bottom corner of her monitor. It read the time: 8:40 pm. Quiet had enveloped the room and she shuddered as the memory of the mysterious figure in the hoodie floated back. She shook even more when the thought crossed her mind that it might be Tony.

She blew out a deep breath and stretched her arms and legs as she yawned. With everything else all set to go, they only needed to wait on the court date to arrive for Mrs. Mason.

She reached for the mouse to shut down her computer when the YOU'VE GOT MAIL box appeared on her screen. A smile lit up her face with the hopeful expectation it would be Kelly, but then fear replaced hope when the memory of their last encounter entered her mind. She still hadn't heard from her friend since last week after they met up for the "game night" Kelly had wanted so badly.

Lauren finally said something to Kelly about Tony a few days after that night. She knew she had to let go of the hoodie discovery, but she couldn't shake the sick feeling in the pit of her stomach, so she spoke to Kelly about it. Unfortunately, the conversation didn't end well and Kelly had since avoided her. She accused Lauren of jealousy, an idea Tony had previously cultivated. Lauren couldn't blame Kelly for the assumption. She couldn't even get Kelly to tell her the color of Tony's car. She was far too livid that Lauren even asked her when she realized why she asked her.

She grabbed the mouse with nervous anticipation, worried about what her best friend might have to say. She finally clicked on it with eyes squeezed shut.

One eye at a time she peeked at her computer. A mixture of relief and disappointment as she saw it wasn't Kelly, but another unknown email address.

A new concern took over as she remembered the last unknown email address and the eerie message enclosed within it. She tilted her head from left to right and stretched her neck out. She breathed out slowly, like a balloon deflating, and leaned forward. Resting her chin in one hand, she drummed the fingers of the other hand on the desk. *Maybe I don't open this one. Maybe I just go home and deal with it in the light of day.*

She clicked on it anyway.


```
Done for the day already? Think about
what advice you give out. It could be costly
to your wellbeing, especially when there are
many late nights you are at the office
alone. Like right now.
```


She froze in mid thought with panic, as she read the email. Her mind reeled on what to do next. *Is there anything I can do? Is this an idle threat or is this for real?* She blinked furiously at the screen to be sure she read the message right.

Someone watched her and this someone did not like her. Briefly, her mind went straight to Tony, but she dismissed the thought just as quickly. Her friend already cut off communication. Not only would more accusations make the situation worse, but also, Tony had won. Kelly had chosen him over Lauren.

Terror wrapped its cold fingers around her throat. She

nervously glanced around the room as she tried to catch her breath. It could be Mr. Mason, but why her, she puzzled. She wasn't the attorney on the case. Still, she wondered if Beth had received a similar email.

Her fingers struck the keys swiftly as she logged into Beth's email account, skimming through the messages in her inbox. She didn't see the address anywhere or any other strange email for that matter. She didn't know when her hands began to shake, but for a moment she struggled with the mouse when she tried to navigate back to her own email.

Lauren stood up, switched off the little lamp in her office, and gazed up at the windows to see if she could figure out where he or she spied on her from. She thought of the last few weeks and the mysterious lights at home and work. With only one window where she could be seen through, the window next to the main office door, she wondered if her admirer also carried a flashlight.

She normally left her own little office door open as well as the main firm door unlocked

Her heart pounded in her ears as she stood up slowly and walked towards the door. Her legs wobbled underneath her, and her trembling increased. Her body reacted before her brain. Lauren panicked that at any moment an evil face would appear in the window or the door would burst open with a mysterious figure that lunged at her. She neared the door and jumped forward to lock it as quickly as possible, but she fumbled due to the uncontrollable shaking of her hands. When she secured the lock, she still shook as she backed up toward her office again. She knew she had to call the police, but worried that if she picked up the phone the mystery stalker would know.

She didn't know how long she had stared at the door when she heard her computer ding that familiar ding again. For several minutes, she tried to ignore the sound that beckoned, though her heart had leapt when she heard it. Part of her felt it could be a trick to get her to look away from the door and a much larger part of herself felt a sense of hysteria about what the message might say. She worked up the nerve to edge herself back into her office, more afraid of an imminent surprise attack that a new message might warn her about.

Once back in her office, she leaned over her computer. Everything moved in slow motion, yet all her senses seemed heightened. Her ears buzzed, a familiar sound that only occurred in a dead quiet. A noise she felt sure would make it impossible to hear what she actually needed to hear. She feared she would drown out all the important sounds. The sound of footsteps or a squeaky doorknob.

She clicked on the message box and the ambiguous email address appeared once again. She held her breath and double clicked on the message...*why am I even doing this?*

```
    Ha ha ha ha ha ha ha ha!!!!!!!!!!!!!!!!!
Did I scare you?????? Good!!!!!!!!!!!!!!!!!!
```

He toyed with her, but by doing so he only confirmed he still watched her. She had to call the cops. Even if he got in here and did some serious damage, she had to do something. She slowly sat down. She wanted to give the appearance that she might be preparing a reply. With her cell phone in hand and her back to the door, she palmed the phone in her lap. She kept it hidden from the view of the door and partially under her desk. Lauren punched in 911 and pressed the speaker icon on the phone.

"911, what's your emergency?" the voice seemed to echo and bounce off every wall in the office. It had been so quiet. She winced, fearful her "stalker" might hear the operator.

"I'm receiving threatening emails at work. I get the impression that this person isn't that far from me right now and I'm freaking out. This person has also made it clear that they can see me, even now," she whispered. She hunched over in her chair in the hopes that sound would become trapped under her body and stop it from escaping the office walls.

"Ma' am, okay, what is your name and location? We'll send a unit to you. Is this person near you now?"

"I really don't know. Most likely. I'm in a locked office at 552 West Harriet, Roseville, Suite 800. My name is Lauren Donlan. Please hurry."

Another ding.

"Please. I think he just sent another message," she said with notable alarm in her voice.

"There is a unit in the area and it should be there any minute. What does the message say?"

She paused while she opened it, then proceeded to read it aloud, "You should be more worried about your client, than yourself."

"What client ma'am?"

"Umm… I don't know. I have a lot of clie--but," she realized, "I have a new client and the situation is bad. We are a family law office. This client is getting a divorce and I'm the paralegal assigned to the case. I had just completed an Order of Protection that's going to be filed tomorrow. Should we check on her too?"

"We have someone out to you right now. They'll be there any minute."

"But what about Mrs. Mason, I think she is in danger," her voice quaked and squeaked. She almost didn't recognize her own hysterical voice. The voice on the other end of the line tried to soothe her.

"Ma'am, can you give me her information and I'll send someone out to her, as well. They can do a welfare check."

After she passed along the address to the operator, she no longer paid attention to her. She would nod her head every few seconds, but then realized the operator couldn't see her when she heard "Ma'am. Ma'am. Are you still there?"

She began to respond with a "yes" or a "no". This went on

for about ten minutes. The operator continually tried to engage her in conversation to keep her distracted and calm. She didn't know what the kind voice on the other end of the line said after a while. She simply stared at the door, waiting for the police or an attack. *Was this shock? Is that what this was? Would I even know if I was in a state of shock?*

Her heart thudded vehemently against her chest and she gasped. She shrieked and dropped the phone when something loud pounded against the front door. She saw a figure cloaked in shadows and dark clothes just outside the window.

"Ma'am! Ma'am! Are you alright? Please answer me if you are alright," she could hear over the speakerphone.

As she adjusted her eyes, she realized the dark clothing resembled that of a policeman's uniform. She sighed loudly and picked up her phone. Lauren walked to the door as she continued to speak with the operator.

"Yes, I'm sorry. I think it's the police. Sorry. He just startled me."

"That is perfectly understandable ma'am. So, you're okay? Alright, I will let you go once you verify it's the police officer and then I will let them handle it from here."

"Thanks."

Lauren still trembled worse than before and she hoped her legs didn't give out beneath her before she reached the door. She refused to unlock the door until she got a closer look at his badge and could verify the number with the operator. He obliged. Suspicions crept in and she welcomed them this time. Even if the officer thought of her as some silly woman who called because of a loud noise, she simply didn't care anymore. She opened the door with some hesitation as she hung up with the operator.

"I'm Officer Taylor. My partner, Officer Martin is checking around the building right now. Can I come in?" he asked as he stepped into the office. She nodded, but didn't know what to say.

"Are you alright? Can you tell me exactly what happened?" he asked. He glanced around for a moment and finally his eyes rested on the wall. He reached over and flipped the light switch on by the door. She blinked at the bright lights, and chided herself silently. She hadn't even registered the darkness of the office. She cleared her throat and chose to ignore her own foolishness.

"Yes. I'll start from a couple of weeks ago, but before I forget, he also threatened my client." Chills took over her body when it occurred to her that even in this dark office, the mystery person was still able to see her inside. She turned her attention back to the officer, whose mere presence made her feel a bit safer.

The officer stood half a foot taller than Lauren and sported salt and pepper hair with pale skin. Lauren guessed him to be in his mid to late forties. He had some lines around his brown eyes, which rested under thick eyebrows. A larger nose sat over a thin slash of lips. He had the start of a pudgy midsection, but looked like he would be able to keep up with the bad guys as his arms were still well muscled. Lauren could only guess his legs were equally in shape.

Before she led him to her office to show him the email, she quickly gave Tracy's information again. She adamantly insisted they check up on her. When she didn't let it go, he checked in over his radio and assured her another officer was on her way to Mrs. Mason's shelter.

She directed his attention to the computer and went through all the details she could remember. From the latest divorce she worked on, to a rundown of all the emails she received. She poured out everything she believed to be relevant. He nodded and scribbled frantically on a small pad of paper to keep up with her. It seemed to take forever and when his partner joined the conversation, forever turned into an eternity. When she rehashed the details several times over, the two stepped away from her and conversed privately.

Lauren decided she should call her boss and let her know what had occurred. Beth shrieked into the receiver and insisted she would head into the office right away. The officers turned back around to her again and waited to ask more questions. To get Beth off the phone, she had to accept the fact she would be coming in to help her.

Officer Taylor's partner, roughly ten or so years his junior, stood equally as tall as he did, but unlike him, he had a very slender frame. He had blue eyes and blonde hair, but his hairline already thinned at his young age. He too had a large nose, but more beak-like with a chin that seemed to disappear under his small mouth. He held his policeman's cap under one skinny arm as he wrote things down on his own pad.

Lauren lost patience with the repetition of the questions and exhaustion set in. In the back of her mind, she still fretted about Tracy's safety. *How long does it take them to get there and report to the officers that she's fine and all's well?*

As she gnawed on a fingernail anxiously, she tried not to rub her eyes, which stung from the late hour. The clock on the wall chimed 10:00 pm, and she could sense this night wasn't close to being over. Officer Taylor finally seemed to acknowledge the annoyed look on her face.

"Sorry ma'am. By going over the details several times, sometimes people remember details they didn't remember the first time around. It's a necessary evil," he smiled sympathetically and added, "We're almost done, I promise."

"Are you alright?" Ms. Brown bustled over to Lauren's desk and put her arm around her, once the officers gave her the okay to enter her own place of business.

"Yes, I'm fine, or I will be," she reassured her. Beth still donned a gray suit with a deep maroon dress shirt underneath. She came from a late client dinner she had been attending earlier in the evening, which made Lauren feel better knowing she didn't get her out of bed for this. For a moment, Lauren thought how nice Beth looked and how she should wear maroon more often.

Her boss patted her head and cooed over her when both officers' radios went off at the same time. Lauren strained to hear what message came across as the radios crackled, but Beth continued to fuss, drowning out the voices. She frowned when she could only make out a couple of useless words, however, their expressions filled in the words she didn't catch. A new surge of anxiety coursed through her veins while she waited for them to talk to her.

Taylor turned back around, after whispering to Officer Martin, "We would really like it if you came to the police station to do an official report and speak with some detectives."

"What happened?" she whispered. She felt her throat constrict. She already knew the answer though. Something had happened to Tracy.

"I'm sorry, but the other unit that went to do the welfare check on your client found her. I'm really sorry ma'am, but she is dead. They are investigating it as we speak, but that's as much I can tell you right now. As a precaution, and to help us with the investigation, we really need you to come into the station with us."

A gust of air hit Lauren as Beth fell into Lauren's chair behind her.

Lauren barely nodded in response, and with robotic motions, stood ready to follow them.

"It's gotta be her husband." Beth stared off into space, but then shook her head. "What do you need from us?"

"Actually, if you would not touch anything in this office for now, that would be great. At least, til the detectives can take a closer look at things. Also, if you could lock up as we leave, that would be best, for your safety. We are having another unit wait here for the landlord, but if you can meet us at the station and answer some questions, as well, it would be greatly appreciated," Officer Martin stated.

Beth agreed and followed the officers when they motioned they were leaving. Lauren felt a sense of relief. She just wanted to get as far away from the building as possible. Beth pushed her toward the door behind the police, so even if she wasn't in a huge hurry to leave, she couldn't dilly dally if she wanted too. Beth followed them out of the office and locked the door. By the time, Lauren and the officers were pulling out of the parking lot, Beth exited the building. She assumed she would see her soon enough at the police station.

She sat comatose in the back seat of the squad car. Fear not only removed her from her office, but she no longer had any desire to return. Initially, the threats frightened her, but somewhere in the back of her mind, she assumed she would be safe. It hadn't fully become real. These threats only came through her computer, after all. Moreover, there were only a few messages. She just didn't understand why she had become the killer's target. Perhaps now that he had finished off Tracy, he would lose interest in her. *Well that's a horrible thing to think.*

She assumed Mr. Mason killed his own wife based on the file Beth had handed her. She stifled a laugh that threatened to bubble up when she remembered at one point she thought it might be Tony sending the messages. However, she couldn't fathom her friend dating a dangerous killer. Besides, Tony would have nothing to gain from this death anyway.

Hundreds of non-stop thoughts swirled in her brain and swooped her away from reality.

As they merged onto the freeway, the events of the evening unfolded in front of her. Tracy was dead. Probably murdered. She swallowed hard to keep the vomit down. *What's gonna happen next? Am I next? How would the police protect me?* She hoped Mr. Mason only contacted her as a way to express a cry for help.

"I, uh…do you think I have something to worry about or was this his way of confessing to his crime? I mean, we've been threatened before, but not…not like this? I'm worried…I mean is he blaming *me*…I'm just the paralegal…, you know, I just … Am I next? is really what I'm asking here."

"Calm down, just try to relax." Officer Taylor's voice went liquid and it had the effect he was aiming for. She felt soothed and assured, though he hadn't said much. "The best people to answer all of these questions will be the detectives. If they feel you are in danger, don't worry, they will protect you."

"I have a job, I can't … I mean are you guys going to come

to work with me?" she shook her head on the verge of tears as the gravity of her situation sank into every pore of her body. But she just shivered instead. She knew she wasn't making sense anymore. She did not intend to return to her job, but then again, what else could she do? She had bills to pay.

Officer Martin turned around. He must have noticed Lauren shiver when she wrapped her arms around herself tightly.

"My jacket is right there, if you're cold at all.," he nodded toward his jacket to the left of her.

"No, I'm fine." She bit her lip and slumped back against the seat, hoping that this night didn't take as long as it already had. She closed her eyes tightly, so tightly she saw stars. *This is just a bad dream. I'll wake up and be fine. Just all my paranoia about Tony.* She opened her eyes. Her vision twinkled and blurred, but she still found herself in the back of a squad car, sick to her stomach.

CHAPTER 10

Half asleep, Joshua dropped his hand down on the relentless alarm clock. *Why won't the damn thing shut off already?* He slammed his hand down repeatedly. Nothing. The ringing persisted. Groggily, he sat up and looked over at the clock. The time of 11:00 p.m. brightly glared at him, but the noise came from somewhere else. He had just fallen asleep at 8:00 that night. *Only three hours of sleep.* The ringing stopped abruptly. He wondered if he had dreamt it. He fell back down onto his pillow when the ringing began again. He groaned as it finally sank in what made the racket. Behind the alarm clock, the face of his phone lit up in perfect timing with the ringing. He wasn't sure if he should move, especially when he knew the only calls he ever received were work related.

After it went off the fifth time, he finally decided to get up. He rubbed his face vigorously, and snatched his phone off the table. He didn't want to answer it, he needed rest. By his own admission, he needed sleep. This only further proved how much he truly needed it.

What felt like weeks since he and Gus had gone to Madison's family property had only been earlier that day. Joshua remained on cloud nine from the find of the necklace, especially after several family members of Tanya's confirmed they had never seen it before, nor had Madison's.

Joshua intended to have Tanya's mother establish the age of the photo, but it appeared to be a more recent one. He had to determine if the blood on the outside of the locket belonged to Tanya. If they could tie the girls to the scene, the crime lab would travel out to the cabin and retrieve more evidence before it became lost to the external elements.

Today they had so many great breakthroughs on the case, he worried that this late-night caller would bear bad news regarding the evidence they had retrieved from the cabin.

He sat in his queen-sized bed and picked up the noisy beast. He closed his eyes briefly before he swiped the green phone icon and answered it. He tried to breathe and remember to keep calm, but his defenses were up.

"Hello?" he said with a gravelly voice into the phone.

"Finally. We have a new case for you. I need you in asap."

His Lieutenant snapped into the phone.

"Can't you get someone else to work on this one, I'm running on steam right now?" There was a pause. *That can't be good.*

"It looks like a domestic between the husband and wife. The wife was found dead. You most likely just need to find the husband after questioning the witness. I've already got Gus going out to the body," the Lieutenant stated ignoring his question.

It did sound open and shut. He exhaled with relief knowing this wouldn't interfere too much with his priority case.

"Fine. I'll be in soon."

"Sooner. Your witness is already here. Oh, and she isn't just a witness, she is a potential victim," he barked.

He hung up the phone and wondered how long it had been since his boss had any rest.

He stretched slowly and looked at his beta fish next to his night stand.

"So, Harry, off to work again," he whispered and threw some pellets into the bowl.

Joshua knew the next case that came his way might not be so quick and easy. He needed to avoid any cases that might be time consuming until he solved Madison and Tanya's murders.

He dragged himself into the bathroom and glanced at himself in the mirror to assess the damage.

Guess I won't be shaving quite yet. It's like I'm going for a record.

He splashed cold water on his face and put on a clean dress shirt and slacks. He wavered a little at the sink as he brushed his teeth. Once he was dressed and washed, he headed into the kitchen to grab a cup of coffee. He lifted a cup to his nose for inspection. *Not great, but it will do.* He flushed some hot water in it.

He grabbed the half-full pot of coffee and poured cold liquid into the semi clean mug. As he placed it roughly into the microwave, he spilled some liquid onto the counter top and the top of his shoes in the process.

"Shit! That figures…" He didn't even bother to wipe either one. The microwave beeped to signal its completion, and he impatiently grabbed the mug, though a little more gently, and took off out the back door, slamming it shut.

Fortunately, Joshua being as dedicated as he was to the police department, had purchased a house only five minutes from work.

He hopped into his vehicle and dialed Gus' number on the way in.

"Awake yet, partner?" Gus grumbled into the phone when he answered.

"Hardly. Got anything yet from your end?

"I just got on the scene, but it's messed up. The husband did a number on her. Killed her in the alley of the shelter. Ballsy."

"Any witnesses?"

"Nope. The only reason we even know about her is cause he told your witness. Find out what she knows, Josh, so I can go home and get some sleep. I'll be back in the office soon. By the way, she was shot, so I'm going to see if I can find a witness, see if anyone heard anything. I'm not holding my breath. Most of these women are scared of ex husbands and don't want to stand out by being a witness."

"Fine, but when you're done, go home. Do your report in the morning. I got this. One of us should be well rested anyway," Joshua insisted.

"Normally, I would debate you, but I'm dead on my feet. See you in the morning." Gus ended the call.

After Joshua parked his car, he breezed through the double doors of the second floor that led to where his desk resided amongst the others. Joshua thought he would get organized before he met up with his witness. *What's her name?* He rifled through his pocket, found his notebook, and flipped it open. Lauren. Before he could read her last name, he looked up to see someone seated in front of his desk already. A young woman furiously scanned through a cell phone and chewed on her lower lip. She looked up for a moment as if thinking about something and it didn't take long before all thought escaped Joshua as he took her in. She had softly arched eyebrows over dark blue eyes and creamy white skin. Slightly pink, full lips, but shaped in a feminine pout. *They look soft.* Long, straight dark hair cascaded over her shoulders. The deep blue cowl neck sweater she wore complimented her eyes even more.

Oh, wow...

She uncrossed her legs, dressed in black suit pants, which then jumped up and down in nervous, jittery movements. Her black, high-heeled boots clicked on the vinyl floor. Joshua had seen pretty women before and dated them, but she stood out from the rest for some reason.

"Hey King, you made it in!" The rookie cop, Hanson, came up behind him and smacked him on his back. Hanson drew Lauren's attention to them with ease. Quickly, Joshua wiped the dumb look off his face and glowered at Hanson.

"Yeah I'm here. Still half asleep," he intentionally spoke louder in hopes of disguising the stare. Perhaps she would think he had zoned out versus the truth. He hoped he didn't have drool in the corner of his mouth. She herself seemed to be wandering in her own mind and didn't notice him gaping from across the room.

He furrowed his brow and walked the rest of the fifty feet to his desk. Clumsily, he set his coffee down, "Hi. I'm Detective Joshua King." He made a concentrated effort to look uninterested. Internally, he chastised himself for his schoolboy reaction.

She nodded impatiently, but he saw the fear in her eyes too, though it didn't surprise Joshua.

"I'm Lauren Donlan." She studied him for a moment, almost awkwardly and unsure. "So, what do we do here? I've told this story a few times. I've been sitting here for hours, it feels like. I just really want to go to bed."

She looked down at her phone, rolled her eyes, and then tossed it into her oversized purse.

"Well let's hear it all. I know you have already done this, but I need to do it again. I will have you out of here as soon as I can," he gestured with his hand for her to relax.

Besides impatience and exhaustion, he could have sworn he noticed an annoyance with him when he gestured for her to calm down. She brought an amused smirk to his lips. Here she sat, scared, tired, and anxious, but he saw a fire ignite quite easily in her. He saw a fighter.

I'm staring again. Get it together Josh.

CHAPTER 11

Lauren wanted to burst out in tears. *The night that will never end.*

Her mood further exasperated by the condescension in the Detective's voice and gestures.

"One of my clients has been murdered and the same guy threatened my life, but you expect me to remain calm. Not to mention, I'm nowhere near NOT calm. I'm tired." She rolled her eyes and sighed, crossing her arms in front of her chest with a huff. He continued to stare at her with this look of amusement and arrogance.

"Fine," she relaxed her hands in her lap and repeated the story of her evening for a third time, *(or is it five times?)*. The text messages to Kelly were not included in that count, whom she contacted the moment she climbed into the squad car. She had still been mid-text conversation when Joshua first approached her. Even though he wore a wrinkled suit and hadn't shaved in quite a few days, she couldn't help but find him attractive. Absentmindedly, she thought he had nice eyes.

So absentminded had she become, she typed that very thought into her next message to Kelly.

```
Who has nice eyes?
```

Confused by Kelly's question, Lauren read her previous message. *Oh my God...that's embarrassing.*

```
No one. Sorry. So tired. The detective is
here now, so I'll text you as soon as I'm done.
```

Lauren put away her phone and hoped her face did not glow as red as it felt.

He seemed to take in everything, including the fact that her head bobbed up and down a few times.

"Are you okay?" he wore a bemused look on his face.

Out of frustration, she perched her chin in her hand and rested her elbow on his desk.

"I'm fine, let's just get this over with."

Even after that, there were numerous times he offered her coffee or reassured her it wouldn't be much longer.

"I'm very concerned that this guy targeted you at all. If it's this woman's husband, why would he focus on you? Do you have any other contact with him? How would you describe the nature of your relationship with this man?" His concern seemed genuine on his troubled brow, but she didn't like what she perceived him to be implying.

"I'm not really sure what that means," she snapped. "But no, the only contact I have had with Mr. Mason is a bunch of profanity laced phone calls and me telling him I can't speak with him. And, of course, hanging up on him numerous times."

"Look, I didn't…okay I did. The fact is I have to ask these questions. I wish I didn't have to make this more difficult, but you want to get to the bottom of this, right? These are the not fun questions that will get us the answers, okay?"

"Okay, fine. But again, there has been no contact outside of a few phone calls where he was really trying to get me to tell him where she was. Maybe three times before, I stopped taking his calls and my boss ran interference with his lawyer. Obviously, he blames me for his wife wanting a divorce, but I find it strange that he doesn't equally blame Beth. Where is she by the way?" She shrugged her shoulders in defeat.

"Ms. Brown, from what I understand, has already been questioned, but didn't have much to offer. We just prefer to question witnesses separately. Like you said, it doesn't appear that she is a target. And I agree with you. It would make more sense if she was or your whole office instead of just you," he said flatly. He stared off as if he didn't mean the statement to be directed towards her.

She didn't bother to reply.

He took a sip of coffee, "Are you sure you wouldn't like more coffee?" She noticed his eyes fell on the Styrofoam cup she had been holding for a while. White chunks lay strewn about on her lap and on the desk.

"Huh?" she looked up, "oh ...uh no, if we are almost done, I would really like to use the bathroom." She brushed herself off and dumped the crumbs from the desk into her cup.

"I understand. It's right down the hall, left, and then left again. When you return I only have few more questions for you and then we'll get you home."

She found the restroom easily. The building structure reminded her of an old elementary school. The brick walls painted in a pale white with bland gray bathroom stalls. There were no windows and terrible lighting. *Or do I just look that awful right now?* Her phone sounded off again in her purse as she stood in front of the mirror.

Tony wants to know when we get to meet your new boyfriend. Lol!

Lauren gazed at herself in the mirror after reading the message with confusion. *Boyfriend?*

What are you talking about?

Boy, you are tired. The guy with the nice eyes, of course.

Pffft...Seriously??? What is the deal with this guy?

Yes, I'm just tired. I don't even remember which guy I was talking about.

LMAO! Too funny! Well keep us in the loop to let us know you're okay or if you need a ride or something.

Thank you! I'm fine for now, still at the police station

At that point, she shut off her phone and swayed a bit. She gripped onto the sink, so she wouldn't fall over. *I need to go to bed.* When she returned to his desk, he seemed to dive in just where he left off.

"Do you have any reason to believe that this guy will be able to figure out where you live? We haven't found him yet and the fact that he contacted you after murdering his wife, we want to be sure that you are safe until we do find him."

She shook her head slowly, "I'm not listed," she stopped. "Although, I would have no idea if he's followed me home before," she finished despondent. She rested her chin in the palm of her hands again, "I've never had to be looking for someone following me before."

"Okay, so no threats of any kind before this. What about your family? Have they received any calls that they have made you aware of?"

The pain of an aching heart flickered across her face for a millisecond, "No, my parents are dead and I'm an only child."

"Oh, I'm sorry. Well to be safe for now, I think I'll just have someone drive by every so often. And then there will be someone close by if anything else should occur," he offered lamely. "I would also like to come by your home tonight and just check it over. Make sure everything looks okay. Do you mind?"

"No, I guess not. It would be stupid not to, right?" she shrugged her shoulders and stood up from the uncomfortable chair, hinting that she was not staying a minute longer in the station. His desk sat in the middle of a large open room and the back of the chair she occupied had very little resistance. Everything ached, not just her heart.

She noticed he looked as tired as she felt and a bit distracted.

"Is there anywhere else you would feel more comfortable staying for the night?" He added as he stood up next to her.

She almost stated Kelly, but HE would be there and she didn't want to be stuck with him in the house again. She felt safer at home than there, which struck her as strange. At the back of her mind, gnawed this unrelenting voice about what had occurred on game night. No matter how terrified she felt at this moment, the idea of going to Kelly's home with the possibility of Tony being there, revolted her.

"No, there really is no where I can think of, but thinking isn't my friend right now either," she joked.

"Okay well let's go check it out together. And then we'll get you to bed. I don't mean…you know what I mean," he stumbled over the rest of his words.

"Okay then," she said awkwardly.

He slowly led the way to his car, with Lauren following, but she noticed he didn't look her in the eye for the next ten minutes.

On the ride home, Lauren didn't want to talk and this cop sure wanted to start a conversation. She presumed his chattiness was a product of the embarrassment from earlier, but she was tired and cranky. She stared out the window and hoped he would shut up. *Maybe if I pretend to be asleep?* She rubbed her temple at the site of a headache on the verge of exploding in her skull. *Come on Lauren, he is just doing his job and trying to help. But do I really need to talk right now?*

As she looked around his vehicle, she noted that it appeared he drove his own vehicle. From what she could tell, he lived in it too. *Bah, who am I to talk, it looks like the city dump ran out of space and started using my backseat.* She sighed to herself as she continued to stare off into the distance.

"No answer?"

"Huh, what?" she hadn't noticed he had stopped to give her a moment to reply.

She tried to answer the random questions he threw at her as her eyes drooped. Dark to light. Every time her eyes closed, the horrors of the evening flashed images behind them. Instantly, they would snap open as fear took hold of her, but it didn't take long for the exhaustion to pull them back down.

She no longer comprehended anything he said to her after a while. Just garbled babbling. Her eyes closed and flashes of lights peered through her lids with each streetlight they passed under in a strobing pattern. Darkness and nightmares soon followed as sleep overcame her.

Lauren woke up drenched in a sweat. She flailed her arms wildly as she grasped at the air. A nightmare she couldn't recall had scared her out of her slumber, yet a sickening feeling lingered with her.

Sunlight splashed across her room, but she remained in a fog between dream and reality. She looked around in a momentary panic and fumbled around to feel something familiar. With a fistful of soft comforter, her brain caught up to her eyes. *I must have*

really *been out.*

She looked to the right to see the blinds shut. She remembered she never got around to purchasing and hanging the accented dark brown curtains she spied at the home store. Without the aid of the extra thick layer of window coverings, the light poured through the beige horizontal slats, causing her to throw her pillow over her head as she laid back down.

She looked down and saw she was still in her work clothes from the day before. She was on top of her comforter versus under it. She stretched out her arms and legs, and relaxed back onto her side for a moment. Finally, she sat up again on at the edge of her king-sized bed, facing the daylight. Lauren yawned and spied the time on the clock perched on her nightstand. Bright green flashing numbers, staring at her in judgement.

"Noon?? Wow, that's never happened before," she informed no one in the room.

Still sleepy, she forced herself to move. She knew she wasn't going to be allowed anywhere near the office today. In the light of day, with the memories of the previous evening flooding back, she had no interest in debating that fact. Once the police caught Mr. Mason, she would feel much better, or she would switch careers she thought to herself. She went to her walk-in closet to pick out clothes for the day. As she flipped through the hangers on the metal bar, deciding what to wear, more thoughts rolled through her mind.

How did I get up here? Oh, it was probably that detective, I bet. I wonder if there is a cop in a car outside right now? Maybe I should make some coffee and see if they want any. And maybe I should call Kelly and let her know I'm okay. She might be worried. Wait! Crap! I shut my phone off, I definitely need to contact her.

For a moment, she considered going back to bed when she glanced over at it. She wanted to disappear into the inviting thick white comforter and light blue satin sheets. Then she remembered the nightmares. She clung tighter to the clothes that she almost set down, so she could climb in. A strange noise from the other side of her bedroom door broke her trance.

She crept to her door and pressed her ear gently against it. *Is that someone snoring?* After a few minutes, she shrugged her shoulders, as she heard nothing further. With clothes in hand, she grabbed a fresh pair of underwear and bra from the dresser next to her closet, and headed out of her room to take a hot shower. Another thought that equally appealed to her.

As she stepped out of her room, she almost tripped over Joshua. He sat on one of her kitchen chairs with the back of it up against the wall, but his head was slumped forward, with his chin on his chest. The hallway wasn't very long or wide, so it was no surprise she almost landed on him. The short hallway contained the doors of her room, the guest room at the end of the hall, and the bathroom door opposite her bedroom.

As she let out a startled scream, he snorted and jumped up, and practically knocked her over.

She teetered backward, but with catlike reflexes, he grabbed her arm. In part to catch her and in part to balance himself. She noticed him fumble with his own feet. Still half asleep, balance worked against him.

"It's Detective King! Are you okay?" he sputtered out once they regained their footing. He looked around wildly. Then he squinted and freed one of her arms to grab the back of the chair for extra support. He yawned and blinked.

Embarrassment crawled across her skin. In a clear frame of mind, she still found him attractive, if not more than the day before. She self-consciously thought about how she must look herself in the light of day, and attempted to avoid eye contact, but he clutched her arm. Her face and neck gained more color when she realized he gripped onto the same arm where she held fast onto her plain white bra. The rest of her clothing had fallen to the floor in the confusion, with the matching white cotton bikini briefs resting right on top. *Well of course.* She bit her lip in frustration, but finally got up the nerve to look him in the eyes.

"You startled me, I didn't realize you were still here," she tried to say with confidence, as she stared at his hand. She hoped he understood the point and prayed she pulled off the appearance of not being embarrassed by her own underwear.

He seemed to get her meaning. "Oh..um.." he stuttered

clumsily and gently uncurled his fingers from around her bicep. "Sorry. Your boss called early this morning before I fell asleep. She is not expecting you to be in today. She said for you to take all the time you need and call her next week," he informed her.

"I assumed as much." She feigned disappointment. She didn't want him to see her afraid for some reason. She stubbornly pushed her chin up, "But thank you for staying…so…uh..I have a lot of stuff to do around here now that I have the time, it seems." Feeling extremely uncomfortable with a stranger in her home, especially one that had seen her underwear, her eyes darted nervously around the room. She didn't know how to say "leave" without it sounding like, "get the hell out".

Once again, her pride reared its ugly head and she couldn't stop the snotty attitude that just flew out. She chastised herself internally, but immediately excused herself due to the stress. Not to mention, the close proximity to him made her uncontrollably anxious. She tried not to wring her hands, or play with her hair. He needed to believe she had it all under control. *Be confident or he may NOT leave due to some cop nature of protect and serve. Strong, confident, sure of yourself…*

"So, I imagine you can show yourself out, and just give me a call if you need something else." she picked up her clothing off the floor. Any excuse to not have to look at him after being horribly rude.

Lauren felt a twinge of regret as she heard him suck in a

breath, taken aback by this new side to her, she imagined.

His face teetered on the edge of laughter and a snarl. She could only guess what must have rolled around in his head at that moment, but Lauren prayed he wouldn't share those thoughts. The thought "What a bitch!" flew through her own mind and she couldn't blame him if that were the case. Yet she refused to back down now. *Damn that Donlan pride.*

She cringed internally, waiting for his response.

"Well," he started, narrowing his eyes at her, "It is my job to protect the public. Tax dollars and all." He turned to walk away, but he whipped back around and added, "And, not to mention, I stayed because *you* asked me too," he added last minute with a smirk.

Her jaw fell open and she took a step back in surprise. She did not see that coming. She wanted to slap the smug smile right off his face, but a horrified chuckle fell out of her gaping mouth instead.

"Wha..Unlikely. I was passed out in exhaustion. I had to be talking in my sle…" she felt her hands get wet with perspiration and her cheeks burn red because it sounded much worse to be asking him in her sleep then just half asleep. A flicker of satisfaction passed over his face the moment her cheeks flushed.

"Whatever, it doesn't matter, I'm going to take a shower. Clearly, I'm not asking you to stay this morning, so as I said, you can show yourself out." She headed into her bathroom and told herself to do her best not to slam the door. He didn't need any more satisfaction from her reactions.

She couldn't even figure out what was so irritating about him or why she got so angry in the first place. Her horrible character flaw flared. She didn't need anyone, and she could take care of herself, though she regretted being so harsh. She was rude, grouchy, and essentially ungrateful, and he gave her no reason for any of it. She had already inched herself back toward the door. Head hung down, she reached for the handle to open it and apologize, when she heard him barking back at her from the other side.

"Actually, I have more questions since you should be more clear headed - I emphasize should be - so I guess you are stuck with me for a little while longer, as I am with you." His footsteps pounded on the stairs as he marched angrily down into the living room. Her fists clenched up into little balls and any guilt she had felt moments ago, she absolved herself of.

As she stood in the bathroom, fuming about what a jerk this guy had been, she looked in the mirror. Her mouth fell open one more time, as she took in the entire picture. Red faced with her hair stuck out in all directions and her mascara streaked across one cheek. She lowered her head in further mortification. The levels of humiliation were piling up on her. *Why should I even care what I look like? He's an ass!*

"Ugh!" she said aloud as she slammed her fist down on the

bathroom sink. She then clunked her head down next to her fist because she realized she just gave him another reaction he surely heard.

"Everything okay up there!" he called up with humor in his voice. She envisioned that aggravating grin back on his face.

"Yep. There it is. Well, he is not going to get to me" she said firmly under her breath before getting into the shower.

"Fiinnne," She retorted in a feigned, happy voice, "just bumped into something." She pushed back the curtain and turned on steamy hot water, hoping to wash him out from under her skin.

CHAPTER 12

Joshua stormed down the stairs of the two-level townhome and fumed. He balked at how easily she pissed him off. However, he balked even more because he let her.

"What the hell? What a bi…!? No I'm not gonna say it, but I come here, do my job, carry her not so light butt into her house, and put her into bed, and then sleep on that uncomfortable chair and I don't even get a thank you!? Seriously?"

Breezing through the kitchen, he headed straight for the patio through the sliding glass door to get some air. His dress shoes clicked on the white tile of the kitchen floor.

He felt steam shoot out of every orifice on his face, which blazed red. His eyes surely glowed to match. He slid open the door and shielded his eyes from sun that sat high in the sky. Everything beamed with happiness and cheeriness. Birds sang and the sun shone. All the foliage looked green and fresh, however, Joshua seemed to instantly dampen the mood as soon as he stepped out onto the cement slab.

The sun blinded him so much his head ached immediately. The condition in which he found himself in made him want to shoot the damn musical birds. The more they sang the more his shoulders jutted upwards toward his ears and the more his head ached. *Nails on a chalkboard, just like her.* As they continued to torment him with song, his skin felt the chill in the air. The deceitful sun tricked all of them and his coat still hung over a chair inside, but he continued to bristle.

He ranted internally about the awful woman he had just met and glowered toward the upstairs window when he heard the water turn on. He paced around the small five by five patio, which seemed pointless. *She has no furniture on this damn thing?*

That's when he noticed a gardener, who *had* been raking up the leaves in preparation for the winter, stop mid-way through pouring them into a bag to stare at him. He also became aware of the fact his internal rant turned into an external one that all those within earshot could enjoy.

"What!?" he glowered at the man. The gardener quickly looked away and finished bagging up the pile in a large black plastic bag. He wasn't sure if it was the stormy look on his face or the hoarse, but awfully loud and hostile sound of his voice that startled the worker. He set his hands on his hips and his right hand grazed his gun holster. *Ahh…That could be the reason he was spooked. Dammit.*

"Hey," he yelled out as he flashed his badge at the man. The man just responded with a thumbs up gesture before he bustled away to the next house.

He still made faces and talked to himself when something in the kitchen caught his eye on his last circle past the door. Something he hadn't noticed before when he had walked by in a rage. All other thoughts ceased to exist as he stopped in his tracks and cautious curiosity took its place. He reached for the door handle and for his gun at the same time. All his rage turned to dread as he saw giant, black, bold letters on the granite back splash. Most likely written in magic marker, he suspected. In all capital letters, he read the message as he passed by and scanned the living room with his weapon ready.

YOU CAN'T GET AWAY FROM ME, I'M EVERYWHERE.

Thoughts raced through his head. *Was this here last night when we came in and I didn't see it? Was it left while we both slept upstairs? Is he still in the house? It couldn't have been here. How on earth would I miss it? I wasn't angry when I first entered last night, surely, I would have noticed. But I came through the front door and I was carrying a load...*

Too many unanswerable questions. He moved to the stairs

quietly. He took note of how empty her walls were except for some trendy, but nondescript wall fixtures. A red metal art deco piece with geometric shapes contained within a rectangular frame on the kitchen wall. More art deco paintings in beiges and browns hung above her couch. The only photos on the wall leading up the stairs were of her and what appeared to be a friend or a sister. He wasn't sure. Her room, though a bit of a mess, had most things in their proper place and she had the most basic of furnishings. He felt a kinship to her and it dawned on him her life in some minute way paralleled his own. There were no plants, patio furniture, and not even a kitchen table.

He continued up the stairs to search all the rooms thoroughly with the hopes Lauren would be none the wiser. He peered around the corner and let his gun lead the way. It took only a few seconds to search the loft. The doors to the rooms were open, except the bathroom. Lauren still showered. He crept forward listening for any other sound.

After searching both rooms, closets, and under the beds he opened the laundry room, which was more of a closet then a room, next to the bathroom. Nothing there either. He moved back down the stairs and did the same in all those rooms and checked all the door locks to be sure they were still engaged. They were, except the patio. *Was that locked when I stormed out?* He couldn't remember.

Finally, he found the garage door off from the kitchen.

Joshua carefully opened the door with his weapon brandished. He controlled his breaths as he swung his arms to the left side of the room and swept back to the right. He scanned the wall for the light switch on the right. Success. He briefly surveyed the large two car space. It sat bare while her car remained in the parking lot of her office. She would need to get it sooner rather than later. Maybe he should get it, he wondered.

He knew she could no longer stay here. Mr. Mason did know where she lived. He took a deep breath as he mentally prepared for the nightmare he imagined the coming conversation would be. He holstered his gun, shut the garage door, locked it, and headed back in with his head down.

While he waited for the sound of the shower to end, he pulled his cell out of his pants pocket and called Gus. They were going to need protection for Lauren, and he needed to know if he had any new leads from the Mrs. Mason crime scene.

"Good morning! You missed out on some excitement here at the Donlan abode. Any new leads on your end cause it's only gettin' better over here," he said as soon as Gus picked up his phone.

"Yeah, I don't have great news and actually was about to call you about that," he responded grimly.

Joshua braced himself for the bad news headed his way.

"Okay, give it to me…"

"I guess it's not great news, but not bad either. Mr. Mason

was found early this morning."

It sounded like good news to him. Joshua realized Mr. Mason must have left his message last night before he arrived with Lauren. He tilted his head back and mouthed the words; *thank you* to the ceiling.

"Great! That means he must have been at Lauren's before I got her home. He left a note here that I j…

"He's dead, Joshua. Before you ask, it does look to be a self-inflicted gun-shot wound."

"Are you sure?" he said with faint relief.

"We won't know for sure until the autopsy is complete, but that's what the crime scene unit believes at this point. We don't know exact time of death yet either."

"Is there anything else before I head back in?"

"He was found in the front seat of his car, a mile away from Lauren's house."

"What!? Why kill himself if he planned on coming after Lauren? Or is it simply coincidence that he was that close?" Joshua whispered this time and looked up to the ceiling.

"He smelled like a brewery, Josh. I doubt there was much planning or thinking clearly," Gus replied.

"Good point. Okay, well I will wait til she's out of the shower and I'll head back into the station." He regretted the words as soon as he spoke them.

"Oh real—"

"Shut up, Gus." Joshua ended the call.

"Ahem…" He spun around to a voice that came from behind him on the stairs. Lauren's hair was still wet and she wore the clothes she had in her hands earlier. He could smell her strawberry shampoo. *I wish I was allergic to strawberries.*

"Uh, so good news, we found Mr. Mason. I believe this whole mess will be behind you sooner than we expected. Including me." He spoke tightly.

She took the towel she had been holding and dabbed her hair at the ends as she moved toward the couch.

"Good good. I think I'll stay here and take some time--- What the fuck is that!?" She almost sat down, but then she immediately popped right back up and pointed at her kitchen wall.

"Oh, yeah, I was getting to that. First, that will need to be washed off, after I take a picture," he said as he went over to take a photo with his phone. "I realize it looks bad and I do think Mr. Mason wrote this before we arrived last night, but I assure you, he will not be bothering you again. We found him."

"How can you be sure? What if he gets out of jail, you know, posts bond, and comes after me?"

"He hasn't been arrested, but don't panic. He's in custody, in a sense. He's dead, Lauren. He killed himself." He put his hand on her shoulder to reassure her, but she fell back into the couch, towel still in hand.

"Oh, okay. Well thank you for everything I guess," she

murmured, staring into space, then she added, "Do you need me to do anything?"

"Um no, not right now." Concern creased his forehead. "Are you okay?"

Her head whipped up to look at him and then she turned away quickly. *Did she just roll her eyes at me?*

"I'm fine. The guy is dead. Couldn't be better."

He put his hands on his hips. *Man, she cannot wait to get rid of me. Fine.*

"We'll be in touch before this is all wrapped up, but overall, I think you're good to go." He checked his pockets for everything before heading for the door, but then remembered her car.

"Did you need a ride back to your car?"

"Crap! I completely forgot." She popped her thumbnail in between her teeth before she replied, "I'll just have Kelly get me later, you have work to do." At this point, she walked across the room and opened the front door for him.

"Alright then." He stamped down his temper that threatened to boil over at any moment.

As he crossed over the threshold of her front door, he turned and tipped an imaginary fedora at her, then giggled to himself when her eyes shot back daggers.

He started the engine of his car and snorted, "Well, bright side, I never have to deal with her again."

CHAPTER 13

Lauren peered out the window, but then released the blinds when Joshua peeled out of her driveway. *I could have handled that better.* She shrugged her shoulders and messaged Kelly right away about a ride. Lounged on the couch on her stomach, Lauren waited for a reply, but her eyes wandered to her kitchen.

Why did he go to all this trouble? And how on earth do I clean that off the wall?

She grabbed her phone as it danced to the vibration of a message being received. Kelly was on her way. Lauren retrieved her shoes, however, as she laced them up another message came through.

> Sorry I spoke too soon. I can't leave
> work, but Tony said he could come get you.

Ewww and no. She didn't know what to say to her friend, but then she quickly came up with a lie.

> I totally forgot too. Boss lady is
> supposed to get me in a few hours to pick up
> the car. I don't know how I forgot that.
> Long night. Sorry.

She pressed send and hoped Kelly bought it. Lauren twisted a strand of hair in between her fingertips and plotted out her next move to get her vehicle. She supposed she could call an Uber. She didn't really want to disturb Beth. Not coming up with an immediate plan, Lauren went to the kitchen and grabbed a bucket and washcloth from the closet.

"Let's see what takes away psycho writing? Dish soap or window cleaner?"

She filled the bucket with warm, soapy water and glanced out her patio door. She noticed a gardener, who stuffed leaves into a half full plastic bag. He wore a baseball cap, baggy jacket, and work pants. She looked back down at her own work and shut off the water before the bucket spilled over into the sink.

When she dunked the rag into the water, she looked outside

again and froze. She locked eyes with the gardener, or felt like she did. He wore sunglasses, but it seemed he stared right at her. Paranoid from her recent adventure, she dried her hands before pulling her phone out of her back pocket. Lauren nonchalantly lifted her head up. The man had moved on to the next home with his rake and bag.

I must be imagining things or reading into them. He probably wasn't even looking at me.

She shoved her phone back into her pocket and scrubbed at the wall with the cloth. To her relief, it started to come off the white tile with ease. She moved to the third word when her phone buzzed again.

```
Are you sure you don't want him to take
you to your office? Tony's just job-hunting
right now. You've got plenty of time to
cancel with Beth and hitch a ride with him.
```

Since she had begun the endeavor of washing a wall she hit a groove, which gave her a valid excuse. She wanted her wall cleaned, and since she had time on her hands, she wanted to clean her whole house too. The need for space from everything and everyone intensified. It no longer was about her avoiding Tony, but about avoiding everyone.

She moved swiftly from one room to the next. Somewhere inside, it didn't feel clean enough. She tried to erase the last few weeks with bleach and elbow grease, yet it didn't work the way she had hoped. She still marinated in an unclean feeling.

After five hours of scrubbing and wiping, she had a layer of sweat and grime that had coated her hair and skin. Ripping off the rubber gloves that she wore, she threw them and the rest of the cleaning supplies into the kitchen sink. Lauren remembered the strange gardener and shut the blinds to the patio door before she headed back upstairs for another shower. Once in the bathroom, she peeled the moist clothes from her body and turned on the water until steam plumed from behind the brown and blue checkered curtain.

Dusk had fallen on her first day off work. Her house was cleaner than it had ever been and her skin glowed pink from roughly scrubbing at it with hot water and a loofah brush. After all the shampoo and soap had been rinsed from her body, a wall came crashing down inside and she slid down into the tub onto her bottom. The hot water hit her face as she pulled her knees into her chest and sobbed. She didn't know for how long the water had pelted her, but it had become much cooler.

She shivered and reached for the handle to the water, and turned it off, and forced herself to her feet to dry herself.

I can finally relax and really enjoy my tv for a change. Lauren wiped at the foggy mirror, once she was dressed, and brushed her hair. Mid stroke she heard what sounded like a door shut from down below.

She paused and tilted her head. *Like that will help me hear any better.* Her heart thumped hard in her chest and her mouth went dry. She listened for five minutes. When no other sounds rose from down the stairs, she continued with her hair. *I'm losing it.*

She finished brushing her hair, held her phone in her hand, and slowly headed back down the stairs, shutting off lights as she went. Her bare feet lightly took one step at a time and she contemplated wine for dinner. Lauren rounded the counter to head towards the wine rack when she fell backwards and covered her screams with her hands.

The wall she spent an hour scouring with a soapy rag had been written on once more, with a similar message.

YOU CAN'T WASH ME AWAY, I'M EVERYWHERE.

She couldn't move her feet. Nothing worked. *What if he's still in here?* Her head snapped upward to look up at the ceiling. The floorboards above her creaked and cracked. *That's it!*

She grabbed her purse and slipped flats on as she fumbled with the lock of her front door. Footsteps could be heard above her heading in the direction of the stairs. She panicked and couldn't seem to get the door unlocked. Either the bottom lock remained locked or the deadbolt did, but neither at the same time would come undone.

Finally, the door released and she flung it open. Lauren ran out the door, checking behind her for the intruder. As she turned to face forward and watch her step, she barreled into someone and sprawled onto her butt on the ground.

"Owww!" She yelled out upon landing on the hard, cold sidewalk. Then she remembered how she ended up on the ground and tried to scurry away from whoever it was, like a crab on the sand.

"Lauren, stop!" a familiar voice shouted.

She finally paused long enough to focus on the person that spoke. For the first time since meeting him, she felt relieved to see Joshua. She jumped up and put her arms around him and quietly cried and pointed into the house.

"I think he's inside still."

Joshua signaled to someone near the car and Gus walked around. Awkwardly, Lauren peeled herself off Joshua and her face became engulfed with flames.

"I cleaned off the kitchen wall, like we talked about. You know the oon-oon-- one, and it-it's there again. That horrible writing. And I swear, I heard him upstairs. Mr. Mason isn't dead. You guys had to 've made a mistake." The cool air mixed with terror, rocked her with tremors and stutters.

"Breathe," he said softly. "I'm gonna go in and take a look. Gus will wait out here with you." Then he disappeared leaving her at Gus' side.

She continued to shiver under the darkening sky with teeth

chattering.

"Do you want to wait in the car? Heat's on" Gus asked. She only nodded in response and let him lead her to the back seat. She rested in the back for about ten minutes when she heard the driver side door open and she bolted straight up. Her nerves were shot.

"If he was in there, he's gone now. And I did see the writing. Yeah, that's a different message. When did it happen do you think?" He gave Gus a grim look.

"I was in the shower, so ten minutes ... oh...," she paused as she remembered she lost time crying.

"What?" concerned he glanced at her in the rear-view mirror.

"Nothing. I was in there for a while, but I did hear a door shut when I got out of the shower like fifteen minutes ago. But either way, it most definitely was within the last hour. What's going on?" her breathing became ragged again.

"I know this is stressful, but I can assure you that Mr. Mason is dead. He is sitting in the morgue. I just saw him. We had his brother ID him already." Joshua stated confidently.

"Great! Well I would say I'm crazy, but it still doesn't explain why you are even here. And two of you this time?"

Gus gave Joshua a look as if to say, 'you gotta tell her.' Joshua sighed, "You do it."

"I'm getting so pissed off right now. Can one of you tell me what's going on?" She leaned forward and placed her head in between both of them.

"ehem..well I'm Gus, Joshua's partner. Detective Harris. It's nice to meet you." Gus cleared his throat and offered her his hand to shake.

She briskly took it and then motioned for him to proceed.

"And like Josh said, Mr. Mason is in fact dead, but we are here because it's starting to look like he may not have been the one to pull the trigger on himself." He had turned to face her.

"What?" She bit a nail nervously, and then leaned back in her seat. "And…"

"Nothing is definitive. We decided we should come out here and make sure you were okay. I guess we came here just in time."

"So, if he didn't kill his wife, then who did?"

Joshua interjected at this point, "No, it looks like he did shoot his wife and that he was possibly on his way to you, but before he got here someone killed him with his own gun." Lauren's face twisted and contorted at all the news Joshua unloaded.

"We would like to take you into the station. We need to update our Lieutenant. We can't let you stay here, not until we get this all sorted out. Not to mention, we need to start from the beginning with our questions. We clearly need to turn over another rock. Somewhere you met or interacted with this guy," Gus added.

Lauren fell back into the seat of his car.

"I just don't think I can keep doing this." She sniffled as they pulled out of her driveway.

CHAPTER 14

Joshua's open and shut case just blew wide open. A reversal of roles occurred when they arrived at the station as Lauren grilled them with questions. However, they were just as perplexed as she was. How could this woman, a paralegal, a non-high profile person, attract two attackers or stalkers in one year, let alone a lifetime?

As they drove into the station, Joshua kept looking back at her. Not that long ago, he could have rung her neck, but then she ran to him for protection and safety. She clung to him and all he knew after that is he wanted to protect her. Frightened and depressed, he could see the worry on her face when he examined her through the rear-view mirror. He wished he could say something to make it better, but the words eluded him.

After they pulled into the parking lot, they headed up to the Lieutenant's office. Past the swinging double doors, they stopped in front of an office with glass windows for walls. There were a few chairs placed directly outside of it.

"Wait here while we give him an update and we'll call you in when we are ready for you," Joshua said as he pointed to one of the chairs.

Lauren fidgeted in her chair outside Lieutenant Jake Halverson's office. With her purse in her lap and phone in her hand, she began to text away. She glanced up every so often to peer through the glass windows into the semi large room. Joshua knew she watched how intently they discussed the current situation, but he also noticed her keen attention to her phone. Her fingers flew across the screen as she typed. He couldn't help but to note how she bit her lip and her eyebrows crinkled in confusion or anger. He wasn't sure. *She has no family to speak of, is she messaging her friend or her boss? Is it this situation that's causing her distress or something else?* He decided he would need to follow up with her afterwards.

Joshua tried to refocus on the conversation at hand with his partner and his boss. This new turn of events where both Mr. and Mrs. Mason were found murdered did not bode well for Lauren. They needed answers. Joshua shifted in his own chair now.

They no longer knew the motivation behind the actions, other than Lauren had to be the link. If Mr. Mason was dead and unable to paint on walls due to that fact, they had little to go on at this point. Did this new suspect intend to frame Mr. Mason or was it all a coincidence? Even more perplexing, if this person had been trying to elude the cops by setting up Mr. Mason, why kill him so soon or at all? Why not hold onto him, or at least attempt to hide the body?

"We need to do a little more digging on this girl. This guy is clearly focused on her. If you want my opinion, if he's willing to take out a "client" of hers, what will he do if he gets to her friends next, and then eventually, her? We also need to sift through which threats Mr. Mason made and which ones this new suspect made? Which one came from who?" Gus chimed in with frustration in his voice.

A large window that overlooked downtown Minneapolis sat behind their boss' desk. Lieutenant Halverson engaged Gus in details regarding the case, as Joshua stared out the window, lost in thought. The office lights of all the surrounding buildings shone brightly, hypnotizing him.

"Correct me if I'm wrong or misunderstanding," the Lieutenant spoke, from a standing position, behind the large oak desk, "Mr. Mason was found in his own car a few blocks down the road from Lauren's home, in the front seat of his own car, shot in the head? And it was made to look like he shot himself, however, it doesn't look like that is possible from what the medical examiner found. And her report won't be ready yet, this is all preliminary?"

Gus nodded as Jake rattled off the details.

"Okay, so tell me something I don't know about this case, guys, other than it's a cluster fuck!" Jake spat with his hands on his hips.

The ruffled Lieutenant, put up a hand to pause the conversation and he went over to the door, opening it, and poking his head through. The entire time Lauren stared at him quizzically. Finally, he shouted down the hall toward the right, "Hansen! Get in here!"

Once the young officer had joined the other three, Jake shut the door again. Lauren went back to her phone.

"I agree with Gus, we have to go through all of her clients. One at a time and anyone else in her life," Joshua offered.

"You sure this is about her and not about the Mason's and this new guy is just trying to throw us off the trail by bringing Miss Donlan into it?" The Lieutenant posed the question to all three of them.

"No motives that we could find. It looks like Mr. Mason killed his wife and at some point, Lauren had attracted a stalker. I feel pretty confident that we're dealing with two different perpetrators. And one killed the other. We can dig further into the Mason's, starting with talking to Ms. Brown if you would like. But again, I say it comes back to Lauren." He nodded in her direction. As Gus spoke, they all turned toward Lauren at the same time, who unfortunately, had also turned her attention back to them.

With ease, they all seem to look away without being too obvious, but Officer Hansen lamely waved at her. Joshua blankly stared at Hanson and then grimaced to Gus who simply chuckled under his breath. Joshua shook his head.

The Lieutenant sat back down in his black leather chair and leaned forward.

"Hanson…what the fu---ugh, forget it," the Lieutenant rolled his eyes and just tapped his pen against the top of his desk before he leaned back.

"Well, you guys need to talk to her about all of this, like you said guys. And let's get these people in here for some interviews. Our focus will be her, but in a completely different light, and before you say anything," Jake waved off Joshua's open mouth, "you will still have time for your other case as well, but you need to start delegating some of your work. Not to mention, before anything else moves forward, you need sleep. It's not a request. Once you discuss with Miss Donlan what's happening, put her in a hotel and you, you get sleep. We'll get some uniforms on her room for the time being. It's gonna take a while before your crime scene labs are completed anyway from the Talbert/Burke case."

The Lieutenant was right. Joshua still needed to wait on the tests to come back and it wasn't going to happen tonight. The funny part, though he had not forgotten about his other case, he felt pulled to Lauren's. Even though she dug more and more under his skin, he felt compelled to protect her. It wasn't meant to be arrogance, but he just didn't feel the confidence in the other officers outside of himself and Gus.

"I can take the bulk of watching her at the hotel. I would feel better if I could. And if something comes up on my other case, then I'll leave an officer with her, like Hanson or Moore?" Joshua posed it as a question, but it sounded dangerously close to a demand.

"If that's okay with you, Lieutenant," he added carefully.

Jake spun around in his chair contemplating the idea as he stared out the window. As Joshua wondered if Jake tempered an angry tirade over his not so transparent demand, he finally turned back around, "Fine. BUT, no overtime." He looked at him, seemingly waiting for an argument.

Joshua shrugged at him and stood up to leave. He thought grimly about the uncomfortable task of how he would deliver this new development to Lauren. He envisioned her face twisted further in annoyance or horror.

Joshua peered through the blinds of his boss' office towards Lauren and pursed his lips. He knew this wasn't going to go over well. Sleep deprivation took hold as he saw things move out of the corners of his eyes. He hovered there, not registering the persistent questions being tossed at him, and then he snapped back to attention when Jake yelled at him.

"Did you hear me!?? Finish up what you can tonight and

then get some rest!" Jake shook his shoulder. He silently nodded his head as he proceeded to the door that separated him from Lauren and a confrontation.

She wore a frown on her pretty face and looked somewhat irritated as she had become engrossed in her phone. One knee bounced up and down as she nervously chewed on her lip. What could be more nerve racking than the current situation she found herself in? He likely read into her body language, but he had to make damn sure they talked about her obsessive use of this phone and perhaps make sure her communications weren't divulging details that might be putting her in further danger. Perhaps, her need for this phone and what it contained, could shed some light on her would be stalker.

She instantly dropped her phone into her purse when he breezed through the door. *Not too conspicuous.* He raised an eyebrow in her direction and stopped right in front of her. His partner stepped behind him, as Joshua spoke, but then faded back a few steps. They had learned over the years it could overwhelm a victim and distress them when more than one of the detectives hovered over them with bad news.

"Gus, here, is going to take you to a hotel. Officer Friendly, over there," he pointed, "aka Hansen, will be there through the night for you, as well. I will be there in about an hour to join the party. In the morning, we can perhaps go over more details about you and your case and the people you have had contact with recently. In the meantime, we all need to get some rest. But I think it's best for you, right now…I mean we think it's best for you, right now, that you not go home. Not until we can figure out exactly what's happening."

He spoke quickly, hoping to avoid questions. Maybe too quickly. He patted the breast of his jacket, looking for his car keys and tried to look as casual as possible. Too late, the skepticism already spread across her face.

"I know what you must be thinking, but before you say anything, we are going to protect you and we are going to find out who this person is. Please trust us."

Her leg bounced again and she launched into a verbal attack.

"What would I need to worry about? That the crack team of detectives didn't realize Mr. Mason was in my home earlier? Or that this crack team didn't realized that it wasn't Mr. Mason, but someone else altogether? Or that said killer was able to find Mr. Mason when you guys couldn't? Or finally do I not need to worry that the same damn people that are promising to protect me right now, is that crack team? Yeah, I'm not worried at all. Pfft." Though her words were vicious and designed to cut, tears pooled in her eyes.

He just shook his head, "Lauren," He tried to be sympathetic and soothe her with his tone, but she just looked away. He sighed and shoved his hands in his pockets.

"I know you are probably scared and angry. And I'm not going to take this personally, at least I'm gonna try not to anyway. We are doing our best, and our best is pretty damn good. However, this is why we need more information from you, so we can figure out who would want to hurt you. And this is why we need to protect you until we do know who we are dealing with."

She looked embarrassed at his light scolding. Her pained eyes stared off into the distance.

"Again, we are doing everything we can. I'm going to retrieve some clothes for you from your home and bring them to you."

A new expression crossed her face. As soon as he mentioned going to her home to get her clothes, she made eye contact with him and her face contorted in disdain.

"I just don't know that I'm comfortable with strangers digging around in my underwear drawer."

"Well, I figured since I've already seen tho…" he cleared his throat and started over when a horrified expression came over her face. He could also feel Gus' eyes on him as well. *Oh great!*

"Look, we all have to do things we don't like right now, but it's to keep you safe. I wish you would realize this," he backpedaled, but he laced his words in sarcasm. She certainly had a habit of missing the point, he thought. G*ranted, maybe this is how she deals with stress, utmost bitchiness. Gah! This woman is maddening.*

CHAPTER 15

Hotel? Mr. Mason is dead and apparently, not the only person I had or have to worry about now. Lauren swallowed the lump in her throat. She started to zone out, and regretted her rejection of Kelly's help, even if it did include Tony. She needed her friend more than ever and she was pretty sure that guests weren't allowed in protective custody.

Toughen up Lauren, get it together…wait, did he just say something about my underwear?

She clutched at her bag and pursed her lips. Ready to follow them to the hotel, she defiantly made it known she hated the entire plan. It remained the last thing she had control over, her own behavior, and she intended to cling to it for as long as she could.

With her best friend lost in a new relationship, she felt alone. More alone than ever. Some mystery psycho was threatening her, the cop on her case hated her, she most likely had a job she could never come back to, and the list went on and on in her head.

As Joshua reached for her elbow to help her up to her feet, she jerked it away. "I can do it myself. I'm not paralyzed," she practically growled. She stood in a huff and waited for them to lead the way, but tears continued to form in the corners of her eyes.

He didn't hide his annoyance with her very well. His whole jaw tightened as he walked away and instantly, she stood taller with pride. She no longer felt the need to cry.

As she followed them through the bright hallway, past two double doors, she wasn't sure how many people they passed and she couldn't even remember getting into their car, but there she sat in the backseat, staring out into the dark evening sky. She tried to look for the stars, but they were hidden from view under a blanket of city lights. She only caught every other thing they said to each other and what they would say to her. She knew Hansen followed them in his own squad car, and they promised to find this guy and keep her safe. Then they were submerged under the dark Lowry bridge on Highway 94. She recognized it immediately.

For some reason, most kids in Minnesota believed this bridge to be a magical tunnel. Adorned with lights on both sides, she dove into a mysterious world where for two city blocks the radios ceased to work while under it. At least back when she was a child. When they burst through to the other side into the dark night, the warm memories faded into the reality she found herself in now. She immediately wished to be back in the tunnel.

By the time she fully snapped out of her trance, she found herself staring out the window of a hotel, and Joshua had already left. Her current bodyguard was Gus, whom she had liked right away. Soft spoken, father-figure type with a sweet dimple in his cheek. Santa Claus without the outfit, white hair, and beard. She smiled at her own imagery. Though she could see he might be younger than her.

Lauren, having finally awoken from her stupor, took in her surroundings. Two queen beds, with nice deep blue comforters faced a dresser with a flat screen TV perched atop of it. A door to her right, led to another room. She vaguely remembered passing through it to get to this room. She stood up cautiously and walked to the window. *This must be a local inn.* She couldn't tell what city it was though. She doubted they drove too far out of Minneapolis. The day had become a blur.

She didn't know what else to do but crawl under the covers and go to sleep. For the second time in the last couple of days, she fantasized about this being a nightmare, one she would wake up from any minute.

Then she did awake, still in pitch black as her phone continued to ding. She found herself covered in sweat and the film of a horrible nightmare stuck to her. *Where am I?* She searched around and located a light underneath the door at the opposite end of the room. It registered where she was, and her whole body sagged under the weight of the memory that flooded back.

Her phone dinged again. *Oh yeah, I almost forgot.* She tried to find the sound and where she had placed her phone. She searched near her pillow and finally grabbed it. As the light illuminated her face, she could see there were twenty or more messages from Kelly.

She pulled the drapes to the window, she didn't remember closing earlier and with the swipe of a finger, she opened the first of many texts. Lights still twinkled from the city, but at this hour, not nearly as many as before.

"Please do not stand in front of the window. It may not be safe," Joshua spoke gently from behind her.

She jumped at the sound of his voice.

"What the hell!?" She whirled around and could see he had opened the door, but she hadn't heard him. *Am I oblivious to everything going on around me?* She clutched at her chest.

"Don't do that! You scared the crap out of me!" she stammered. She sat back down on the bed right away and bent down to grab her phone that she had dropped. "I thought Gus was taking the first shift anyway, didn't you need to sleep or something?"

He scratched his head and rubbed his neck, slurring

slightly, "I'm planning to sleep myself, soon. Took a little bit more time than expected and I got some of your things. Just got back and wanted to check on you. Your bag is in the other room. I'll bring it in before you go back to bed so you can change in the morning."

"Oh. Makes sense," she said. She stared passed Joshua, but then looked back down at her phone again and saw the time was midnight.

"You do know that you can't tell anyone where you are. In fact, are you up to some questions right now or do you just want to wait until tomorrow?" he pressed lightly.

"I wouldn't tell anyone." She balked at the suggestion. "And quite frankly I think we should wait til after you have had your rest, before we start another interrogation. It's midnight, I should go back to bed anyway. I'm still tired just ...." her sentence drifted off.

"Having nightmares?" He finished for her.

She could only nod. The vulnerability that struck her made her angry.

"I know you don't want to answer questions, but I have to ask. Did you tell anyone when you were going to be home last night? Did you tell anyone that you would be working late the night of the murders?" Joshua asked as he sat down on the bed opposite of her.

"No one." She shook her head in confusion. Her mind raced. *Who did I tell? Obviously, Beth would just know, as she is*

*my boss, but who would Beth tell? No one. And who else would I
tell? Kelly, but who on earth would Kelly even tell? She is so
wrapped up in her boyfriend these days, no one else seems to exist.
Okay, I'm being unfair. It's perfectly normal to get wrapped up in a
new relationship. Focus, who else? There just isn't anyone else.*

Lauren tugged at her lower lip and didn't notice she had
begun to pace. As she continued to burn a hole in the carpet with
her quick steps, she tried to retrace her interactions with people
from the previous days in her mind.

At the police station, she had grown even more concerned
for Kelly when she hadn't heard back from her right away. It
wasn't like her to not answer relatively quickly. So, in response to
that, Lauren had sent a couple panicked messages, but then she had
been whisked off to this hotel and forgot to check for responses.
Kelly must now be experiencing what Lauren had and this
conversation with Joshua needed to end, so she could put her
friend's mind at ease. And maybe she would also give Kelly a
piece of her mind for making her worry. *Giving her a piece of my
mind after I just did the same thing to her. That's dumb.*

It wasn't the first time Kelly had been in this kind of
relationship, but everything happened so quickly. Moving in after
only a few weeks, disappearing, and rarely responding to her calls
or texts after the first weeks of dating. It wasn't an urgent worry at
this point, but that game night. She couldn't shake the question
mark over what exactly happened. And Kelly just seemed so much

more lost in this guy than any other before him. *Focus, Lauren!*

Pacing in this hotel, only God knows where, Tony dropped to the bottom of her list of concerns. Tony. That issue paled in comparison. *HOW DID I END UP HERE!!????* She thought of him as a possibility, but it made as much sense as Mr. Mason did initially. She didn't seem to have much of an impact on Kelly and Tony's relationship, so she couldn't justify in her head a need for Tony to even lash out, let alone in such a dramatic way. If Kelly had broken up with him because of her, maybe she could see him fall apart at the seams, but he won the battle for her attention. *It can't be him.*

Startled, she awkwardly ripped her hand away when Joshua gently held it. She flushed red at his touch.

"Sorry, you took me by surprise," she faltered. She wasn't sure why she felt it necessary to give him an explanation for her reaction. *Why the hell is he trying to hold my hand for?*

"I just wanted you to stop, you were making me dizzy," he gently joked.

Oh. Now why is he being so nice? It's making me uncomfortable. And now I'm blushing again. Ugh. It didn't take long for her to realize the depth of his exhaustion. He must be delirious, she assumed.

"Again, I'm sorry. I'll sit. I just can't think of anyone besides my best friend that knew where I was on both occasions. And I really doubt she is a murderer or wants to murder me," she sighed. In the few moments, since he had grabbed her by the hand, she had become aware of the fact they were alone. The air seemed to be sucked out of the room. His need for rest gave her the perfect out. Or him the perfect out. Either way, she wanted him out of the room at the very least. As subtly as she could, she moved closer to the door to open it for him.

"Look, why don't we do the fun questions later, and you get some rest." She pulled it open wider, lights from the other room filled the entry way.

He jerked to attention, seemingly wide-awake, "What's happening?" he spoke roughly for the first time since leaving for the hotel. It threw her on the defense again.

"Oh, calm down, you are going to the next room to sleep. Gus is perfectly capable, as well as that other guy, Hansen. Unless he left when you came back. They are both right outside, right?" she stared at him waiting for a response.

Finally, she let go of the breath she held for mere seconds, yet she could have sworn her lips had turned blue from lack of oxygen. Her physical reaction to him annoyed and shamed her at the same time. Especially, at a time like this. Someone wanted to kill her, someone had killed, most likely because of her, and Lauren explored a different type of knot in the pit of her stomach.

"You are right, Gus is perfectly capable," he winced and added, "Man, that hurt."

"What?"

"Admitting you were right." He winked at her this time before he got up and walked out of the room.

"Pffft!!" Her less than clever retort made *her* wince.

CHAPTER 16

I'm so sorry it took so long to get back to you! What do you mean they don't know who it is? I thought it was your client's husband?

The next morning Lauren sat in the bathroom texting. She had shut the sound off to avoid attention from either detective, while Hansen stood guard out in the hallway of the adjoining rooms.

They continued to text back and forth for a few minutes, with Kelly expressing great worry and concern. Tony, who didn't seem to like Lauren much, now exuded a brotherly interest for her wellbeing. She figured her bestie would be obnoxiously distressed after not hearing from her for hours, but she didn't see the Tony thing coming. She clicked her tongue on the roof of her mouth and looked at the door in the bathroom. A mirror attached to it reflected her own image back.

She pondered what she would be able to reveal, making unsure and judgmental faces at herself. She knew it couldn't be much. It was her best friend though. She responded to Kelly, but her likeness in the mirror scolded her for possibly revealing too much. *It's Kelly and I didn't tell her exactly where I am. Shit. I don't even know exactly where I am.*

She sat quietly wondering if she should do a fake flush, just in case Gus had noticed the amount of time she had spent in there. Her phone vibrated in her hand.

```
You know I won't tell anyone. I just
want to know you are safe. We just want to
know you are safe.
```

Lauren sighed deeply, and before she gave up more confidential information, like the actual address and directions to the hotel, she asked her how things were going with Tony. The subject change worked. Kelly texted back with positive reviews on her relationship and how it seemed to have improved since the last time she and Lauren had spoken.

Lauren finally stood up, relieved her friend took the hint with the relationship questions and sent one last message.

```
    I do appreciate your concern and
checking up on me. I'm sure we'll be in
touch soon, but I better go. They might
start to fear I have fallen in the toilet.
:P
```

She slid her phone into her jeans pocket. She decided to shower and get ready for a day of doing nothing. This would provide a reason for why it took her so long in the first place.

Once she had cleaned up and changed into her sweats she felt a lot more relaxed and came back out to join Gus, who filled out a crossword puzzle while he sipped on coffee. Lauren stretched out the couch next to the big arm chair he occupied.

"Do you mind if I watch some TV out here?" She hoped Joshua would be asleep for a bit longer. She constantly felt tongue-tied and embarrassed around him. It was like being a teenager again, she only lacked the acne.

"Not at all, we have nothing but time to kill anyway. Have at it." He winked at her then looked back at his crossword.

It felt like only a few minutes had passed even though it had been several hours, before Gus and Lauren heard a loud thud from Joshua's room. Without further warning, he burst into the room from the adjoining door. Lauren sat straight up and Gus hopped to his feet ready to draw his weapon. What alarmed her more than him barging into the room, was he wore nothing more than his boxers. Joshua's ignorance of this fact put Gus in a good mood from what Lauren observed. His eyes gleamed and sparkled.

Lauren wanted to avert her eyes, but they gaped at his body while her mouth hung open. He wasn't overly muscular, but she noticed the tone of his body right away. Light brown chest hair covered the upper portion of his body, which trailed down to a point around mid-stomach. Luckily, Joshua hadn't even figured out he stood there half naked. *Thank God!* She managed to look away just before Joshua looked in her direction. When his eyes rested on her, she heard him sigh in relief.

"Shit! You guys scared me! I thought something had happened to you! I woke up and no one was around."

"Scared you? You came out of there like a bat out of hell!?" Gus snorted as his hand fell away from the butt of his gun. Lauren felt Gus gaze at her before he looked back at Joshua.

"Maybe you need more rest, guy?" Gus chuckled as he looked him up and down and then nodded in her direction.

"What time is it even?" Joshua ignored him. A few seconds later, a strange look appeared on his face. Frozen in place, he looked down with hesitation. A quiet groan escaped his throat. Gus shook his head with laughter in his eyes. Lauren blushed---again.

I have to stop doing that! As soon as Joshua looked back up, she looked up at the ceiling. He turned around and went back into the other room.

When he shut the door, Gus laughed and Lauren joined.

"Think he will come back?" Lauren asked Gus. *Please let him come back with more clothes on.*

"Yeah, he's not as shy as he's letting on."

He finally came back out some twenty minutes later. Clothed. Lauren mentally wiped her brow.

He wore this goofy, embarrassed expression which endeared him to her. Also, those long lashes and green eyes and full li--.

Is it hot in here? Maybe they should crack a window or something? Stop! Stop! Stop! Imminent danger, remember.

"Are you okay?" Joshua asked her. He wore jeans and a long-sleeved t-shirt.

She smiled and thought quickly, "Oh um, yeah, just thinking about my best friend. I'm just worried about her." *It's partly true. At least, up until he exploded into the room wearing his...is that Christmas underwear he's wearing?*

She hadn't looked at her phone since she had showered. She feared they might confiscate it if they felt she might divulge their location.

Lauren adjusted the form fitted dark green hoodie she now wore, with her black leggings and thick grey wool socks. She reached for the remote to the TV. *What on earth were they going to do all day? How long would they have to be hiding out in this hotel?* She only had a few items Joshua had brought, none of which included games or anything to do. Luckily, at a hotel they were fully stocked with shampoo and soap.

"What was that loud thud anyway?" Gus asked pointedly.

Joshua scowled at his partner and mumbled something about falling out of the bed.

Once again, Gus and Lauren shared a laugh at Joshua's expense, who just continued to ignore them as he made another pot of coffee.

Still chuckling, Gus pushed himself off the maroon recliner he had occupied for some time. Lauren realized he still wore the same clothes from the day before. With a wife who waited at home, Gus most likely wanted to go for a little bit to see her and sleep. Not to mention, he looked exhausted.

"Well, guys, I'm off. I'm gonna grab you some food and then I'm heading home after that. I'll be back for the nightshift, but Officer Moore will be outside until then, he already relieved Officer Hanson."

Joshua followed him into the hallway. He also greeted the young officer, Moore. He was tall, dark complexioned, in his mid-20s and wet behind the ears. His big brown eyes were kind and put her at ease right away, but his broad chest added a feeling of security. Wet behind the ears or not, Lauren learned from Gus that he scored extremely high at the academy and continued to prove to everyone he intended to move up the ranks quickly.

Lauren sat in front of the TV while they were out in the hall and grabbed her phone nervously, not wanting to be caught, but not sure what would happen if she was. More messages from Kelly had been received in the hours she had watched reruns of Friends.

She quickly swiped the phone awake and read the messages briefly. More commentary about her concern and Tony's. It irked her to read it. And a final message stated she would contact her later because Tony had just arrived to grab her for lunch.

The door cracked open and Joshua was still engrossed in a conversation with Officer Moore. She quickly put her phone away before he could see it.

Lauren could hear Joshua laugh about something with Officer Moore before he stepped back in the room, quietly shutting the door. They just stared at each other in awkward silence for some seconds. She felt an entire ten minutes had surely passed.

How long would Gus take with the food, and then what? She wondered. The only noise that could be heard came from the Family Feud playing in the background. She smiled nonchalantly and stared at the TV as if it were no big deal, but her face burned with heat. She concentrated so hard on appearing uninterested in his presence that she couldn't be sure which family on the show had the lead. She pulled her hair in front of her face, which hadn't been red this many times since high school.

At least being a bitch takes the focus off my face.

"Well," he said after more tension filled minutes had passed, "we are stuck here, we might as well make the best of it."

What the hell does that mean? Could it be worse for him

than I thought? Maybe he has a wife or a girlfriend to get back to and he's stuck with me. Or maybe he just can't stand me that much.

"What did you have in mind?" She sighed lightly. Her color had returned to normal. She brushed her hair away from her face. She wore no make-up, her lips had a natural pink tint. She usually put make up on and did her hair for work each day to make a good impression for the firm, but on her days off, she liked to let her skin breathe.

She waited for him to suggest something, but he had been just staring at her, perhaps through her. Finally, she said it again, "What did you have in mind?"

He seemed to snap out of it and held up an index finger as he searched through the bag in the corner of the room.

"Ah ha!" he exclaimed, almost relieved he found the desired object. He flashed the deck of cards in his hand with this comical look on his face. She had yet to see this lighter side of him.

A nervous laugh bubbled up inside her, and she chuckled at him softly with her head tilted back. She smiled, revealing lots of white, straight teeth. Once again, he seemed to stare at her, and for the billionth time she blushed, but only slightly. Hardly noticeable, she hoped. This time he recovered more quickly and sat down on the couch next two her. *He smelled good, but he hadn't even showered yet that day. NO! Focus on whatever we are going to play.*

"A little war?"

She cracked a smile once more, but attempted to stomp down the emotions that clamored inside her and threatened to spill forth. "Sure."

CHAPTER 17

Her smile. Her laugh. Her voice. *How could one woman be so infuriating and so desirable all at the same time?*

Gus had come and gone during their first game of war. Throughout the day, they played war, poker, go fish, and more poker. Interspersed in casual activities they talked and they talked and they talked and they talked. At first, it broke the awkward silence that clung to the room, stifling the air, but once the conversation took shape and flowed naturally, he realized, they seemed to have quite a bit in common. It had turned seven o'clock in the evening before they realized it, and Gus would be returning shortly.

Joshua had briefly mentioned his sister, skipping over the

awful details. He gave her the short version. She seemed genuinely sad and horrified all at the same time. At one point, she reached out to touch his hand when he spoke of Renee, but hesitated and withdrew it.

"I'm so sorry. Did he go to jail?"

"No. He got away with it. It took me years to let go of that." A mischievous look appeared in his eyes.

"Okay, I may not have let it go. Between you and me I could get in a bit of trouble if they found out that I was keeping tabs on him. More so if they realized I might send him messages from time to time to let him know I'm keeping tabs on him."

"Messages? Might?" she raised an eyebrow.

"Anonymous messages that would be hard for them to trace back to me, but enough to really keep that guy on edge. And I'm sure he knows they are from me. Perhaps if we get to know each other better I'll tell you what exactly those messages said. Which reminds me," he added, "I haven't had a chance to send him any of my love notes since my last case began. I wonder if he misses me?" he mused with a crooked grin.

She shook her head at him in chastising disapproval, but the humor twinkled in her eyes.

Versus an interrogation, Joshua learned so much more about her with just this candid conversation. She told him about her profession and why she chose it and she talked to him about her best friend. It didn't take long for Joshua to see the strength in their bond through Lauren's description. It softened her when she gushed about their friendship. That softness was overshadowed briefly when the conversation turned to Kelly's new boyfriend, Tony. His ears pricked up when she mentioned the odd encounters with him and the accusations he directed towards Lauren. *Mental note, research Tony.*

"It's okay," she assured him. "I am planning to talk to Kelly about this stuff, again. It's just all these other things began going on around the same time."

She finally reached over and squeezed his hand, which took him by surprise. He could only guess his face registered the surprise since she threw her head back in laughter. *Why does she have to have a sexy laugh?*

It wasn't giggly or high pitched and it wasn't too low either. It was one of those laughs that just made you want to nuzzle and kiss her throat. *Man, I'm not gonna survive being stuck in this room with her for very much longer.*

"You just had this look of concern on your face, but when I tried to reassure you, your concern changed to bewilderment and confusion. I know I should be the one that needs reassuring during this kind of time, so I understand why you might get confused." She giggled once more and took a sip of her coffee that had to be luke warm at this point.

"Oh of course. I was confused." He cleared his throat thankful she misunderstood the look on his face, and reached for the cards almost at the same time as she did. When their hands met, she pulled away. *She is impossible to figure out, she just squeezed my hand to try and comfort me, but now this?* He scratched his head.

She had no family except Kelly, again another thing they seemed to have in common, now that Renee was gone. She worked long crazy hours and her job took over her life, much like him. The worst part was he had never felt this much attraction for someone before and he didn't know why. They barely knew each other. She was a magnet constantly pulling him in, though sometimes repelling him. In the short time they spoke, he felt he even more connected to her.

He examined her further, wondering if she felt the same way towards him. He couldn't read her, so he slid closer to her to gauge her reaction. The moment he shifted closer, she moved away.

"So, you and Kelly went to this party and she met Tony there. Did you meet anyone?" he prodded.

"No, I had to work, so I left before he even came around," She moved slightly towards the other side of the couch and it sounded like she stammered a little. *Did I embarrass her just now?*

"Huh, yeah I understand that. I'm always the first to leave a party," As he shuffled the cards, he inched over some more, making it appear as if he simply needed to readjust himself.

He heard her sigh and move again. Inside he chucked, yet

he grew more intrigued.

"Do you want to deal this time?" he scooted over in her direction one last time while presenting her the deck of cards. She abruptly stood up, spilling her coffee onto his lap. *Not luke warm! Not luke warm!*

"Yeow!" Joshua yelled out as the coffee burned his lap and then he followed her lead and flew off the couch, but from the pain.

"Oh, my God, I'm so sorry. I didn't..uh.."

"I have to go to the bathroom," he rushed off.

As he passed the mirror on the dresser, he could have sworn her face took on a pink hue as she buried it into her hands.

When he came back out, she stood up with an apologetic look on her face.

A double knock on the door broke the silence and Gus entered the room. "Ready for that break?"

"Sure, you get the easy one; you get the shift where she's sleeping."

"Yeah the boring one." Gus laughed.

"Trust me, I'd take the boring one." Gus cocked his head in question and Joshua added, "Don't ask." And he headed back to his room, passing Lauren on the way.

"Good night," she smiled curtly.

He turned and stopped, "It's really okay, okay?" he put a hand on her shoulder. Instantly, she moved away from his touch, but smiled.

"I do really feel awful." She then went to her own room. Joshua stepped back into his room and left Gus alone, who took ownership of the remote and began to flip through the channels on the television.

Joshua eagerly crawled into the freshly made bed in his room. However, his head barely touched the pillow when thoughts of the previous days rolled through it, peppered with the mundane to do list of the next day. Although all these thoughts assaulted him he succumbed to sleep within minutes and dreams soon whisked him away. They contorted into nightmares of his sister and floated back into dreams of Lauren. The dream devolved back into another nightmare. The mystery killer closed in on Lauren, and Joshua knew he wouldn't make it on time to save her. Before she released a horrifying scream, his eyes were open and he sat straight up in the hotel bed, breathing heavily as if he had literally been running to rescue her.

He tried to shake the dream off him with a hot shower. He let the water blast him right in the face. By the time he was finished, the dream had faded quite a bit, but unfortunately the sick, foreshadowing feeling, he could not seem to wash off. As he pulled another long-sleeved tee over his head he exited the bathroom. Apparently, he came back out just in time. There was a knock on the hotel door. He looked around and Lauren wasn't up yet, just Gus.

"Room Service!"

Joshua cocked his head at his partner, who just shook his head in denial. Signaling he had no knowledge of a room service order. Gus stood up and both detectives pulled their side arms. Gus stood to the right of the door while Joshua peered through the peephole. It did appear to be room service. They carefully opened the door. The hall was empty save the metal platter left behind on the ground right in front of the door. Odd that the delivery person didn't wait around for a potential tip, as well, Joshua thought.

Joshua and Gus still brandished their weapons. Joshua gripped the handle more tightly when he saw a single white card with no lid on the metal tray.

This guy is going to a lot of trouble just to fuck with us.

They remained in the hallway as Gus opened the envelope. Another note from the mystery man.

YOU CAN'T HIDE FROM ME, I'M EVERYWHERE.

"Who the hell is this guy, Gus?" Joshua gritted his teeth in exasperation. And once again his partner could only respond with the look that said he had absolutely no clue.

"Where's Hanson or Moore?" Joshua spat angrily. His whole body shook. Then he peeked into the crack of the door. He could see Lauren staring at the TV. She had awoken and come out. He hoped she hadn't heard anything.

Hanson popped out of the adjoining hotel room, straightening his gun belt.

"What the fuck dude? Where were you?" Joshua poked his finger into Hanson's chest.

"I had to use the can," he stammered and stepped back.

"You talk to him. I'm going to do a perimeter sweep." He said to Gus with his back to Hanson, then he turned to face the rookie once more, "Hanson, make sure there is someone out here at all times! Got it!"

Joshua then walked carefully down the hallway to the main entrance. His gun back in the holster, but his hand rested on the butt, ready to draw it out if necessary.

He heard Gus lecture Hanson some more. However, before he turned the corner, he saw Gus was on his way to check the other end of the hall.

Let's go talk to the fucking front desk.

After he questioned the front desk clerk, and was certain her stalker no longer roamed the halls of the hotel, Joshua headed back to the room knowing that once again they had to leave.

Gus waited outside the door and before they headed back into the room, Joshua put his index fingers to his lips, indicating to Gus not to mention it to Lauren. If the killer wanted to get to her, he could, at least that's the message he sent.

So, what's the game? How did he find them? She had finally calmed down last night. She deserved 24 hours without bad news, if he could help it.

They walked back in and Joshua smiled at her puzzled and fearful face. She clutched her phone so tightly her fingers had turned white.

"Nothing to worry about. It was just a mistake in the room number. They were trying to deliver next door. Boy, did we give him a scare though," he reassured her as he patted his side arm.

"You were gone a long time for it to be a mistaken delivery." Her eyes narrowed.

"Well, yes, but we did have to look around and question the front desk to be sure. It's fine now, okay?"

The look on her face made it clear she wasn't buying his story. Luckily, Gus quickly changed the subject.

"I'm gonna check in with Lieutenant Halverson and see where we're at with the case and if he needs anything else from us, or you, as far as information, whatnot. Maybe *they* have some information. And we can grab something to eat too. I'm famished," Gus stated as he patted his belly and headed back into the hallway with his phone.

"Not smooth or believable. At all," she said looking at Joshua but nodding toward Gus and his attempt to distract her. "What is really going on?"

Joshua was going to respond, but he remembered the phone in her hand.

"Have you been messaging anyone today?" He pointed at

her cell phone in her hand.

"Uh, it's just my friend Kelly. She is worried, I had to answer. She was blowing up my phone," a scowl spread across her face at the line of questioning. This woman infuriated and intoxicated him all at the same time.

"Did you tell her where you were?" he quipped.

"She is my childhood friend since we were three years old. I sincerely doubt it's her," She rolled her eyes at him. And she added, "And no, I didn't tell her, even though she pressed and I feel like a terrible friend. The only thing I told her was the city we're in, or appeared we were in since I don't know for sure. She isn't a super sleuth."

"Okay, I just wanted to be sure. I know this is hard, but if she is your friend, she will understand that it's for your safety. Let's get our stuff together, I want to find out what happens next."

"I knew it!" She jumped up. "'What happens *next*?' What happened first!? Was that really room service or another threat? Tell me what's going on. My whole life has gone to crap in the last couple of months. This is about me don't I deserve to know what's happening?"

She had begun to pace again and the color left her face. *Usually she was red, so it seemed.* He didn't want this all to come crashing down on her again, but they did have to leave and soon. Instinctively, he grabbed her again, but by the shoulders this time. She tried to pull away, but he wasn't letting go.

Tears formed in her eyes and her breathing had become erratic, so he wrapped his arms around her to calm her, to keep her from moving. Surprisingly, she didn't fight him. She went limp, head shoved into his chest, and she took a deep breath, a relaxing breath. When he stroked her hair to shush her, she relaxed further into his arms with a sigh. He teetered on the verge of rocking her, but the scent of her hair caught his attention, and instead he pressed his lips gently to the top of her head. He breathed in the sweet smell and he felt her tense up immediately, but didn't raise her head. *Dammit.*

It's for the best anyway. Joshua realized Gus would be walking back in at any moment and he didn't want to deal with the grief he would get from him, so he gave her a gentle pat on the back before pulling away. *Mmmmm, her hair smells good.*

Attempting to squash his feelings for her proved most difficult. He looked down and intended to direct her toward the couch and have her sit and relax, but he noticed she was red again. At first, he felt mystified. She wasn't looking at him yet, but he cocked his head as if some mystery finally unveiled itself to him. It began to register why she constantly blushed since the day she arrived in the station. *Some detective I am.*

Their eyes met as she lifted her head. However, she too appeared to be reading his expression and equally registered his revelation. Her eyes widened slightly and she took a nervous step backward. He instantly countered her move like a chess game and took another bold step toward her. Before he could do what he wanted, what he was sure they both wanted, Gus barged into the room. *A kiss would have to wait.*

Gus still examined his phone as he spoke, "We're hitting the road. Another uni ..." Gus trailed off, when his eyes found the pair in the room. Reading the body language in the room, he casually glossed over Lauren, who had a guilty expression on her face. He rested his eyes on Joshua who rolled his at him before Gus finished his sentence... "Hmmm... as I was saying, another uniform will come by to collect our belongings right away and meet us at the next hotel." He smirked. *Smug son of a bitch.* Joshua grimaced inwardly.

Joshua turned back to Lauren, assessing her once more before barely whispering, "We'll finish this later." She swallowed hard and once again her cheeks flamed with color.

Joshua rubbed the back of his neck. He knew he didn't hide what almost happened from his partner, but he sure as hell was going to try and pretend nothing almost happened as he said to Lauren more audibly, "I'll explain our current situation when we get back to the station, okay? But right now, Gus is right, we have to go."

She nodded. Through her embarrassment, he could see anger behind her eyes too. She exhaled and released air she must have held onto for their entire exchange. Lauren avoided eye contact with him. They got into her into the car, but they both spun around and stared Hanson who rushed toward them at full speed with a piece of paper in his hand.

"I found this on my windshield. He has been following us. That's how he found us," he sputtered out of breath.

Joshua placed the note in a plastic bag he retrieved from the drunk of his car and then read it.

I'M EVERYWHERE...

"Let's divulge all of this to her after lunch, shall we? We'll pick up some food to go and then eat at the station. If he's following us, it's safest at the precinct." Joshua said as he shoved the plastic bag containing the note into his jacket pocket.

After they picked up some food through the drive thru, they head back toward Minneapolis, back through the dark Lowry Bridge Tunnel. It was nearing mid-afternoon and they hadn't gotten any further on this case since they had picked her up a few days ago. However, it seemed that Lauren's stalker certainly made progress and was closing in on her.

Joshua watched her in the rearview mirror, just staring out the window, playing with her hair. It didn't appear she focused on anything in particular. He could only imagine what went on in her mind right now. From time to time, their eyes would meet in the mirror and she would instantly look away. *Did she just roll her eyes!!?? Good! I'm starting to understand you a little better, Lauren.*

Since their first meeting, she sniped at him or blushed

because of him. He began to read her for the first time. She seemed to react this way when she became nervous or, from what Joshua could tell, flustered. And he definitely flustered her.

He looked out into the overcast day and the trees were almost bare. A chilly breeze coaxed the dead leaves down the street. Joshua frowned. He couldn't help but feel as if Mother Nature was trying to warn them of something coming.

CHAPTER 18

Awesome. What's he looking at anyway? From the backseat of Joshua's car, she grew more and more irritated with him. Especially after their little interaction at the hotel. *How dare he? That arrogant look on his face as if he knew something I felt or thought. Ugh! Of course, he's not wrong, which is hardly the point...* She rolled her eyes at his smug look in the review mirror. *Dammit, he just caught me looking at him again...Ugh.* Her stomach fluttered. She looked down and shook her head at it, scolding its betrayal.

While they ate their lunch in uncomfortable silence, she received another message from Kelly. She made sure to show them everything that she said to avoid further issues in the future. Kelly, simply wanted to know how she was doing and Lauren let her know that she was no longer at a hotel but back at the station. She couldn't explain right now, but would in the future.

Before they knew it, it was 200 pm and they were headed up to Lieutenant Halverson's office again. Stuffed from lunch she needed a nap, but it seemed a chair would have to suffice. The weird tension between her and Joshua dissipated as she felt the walls of the hallway close in on her and swallow her whole. The uncertainty of her future made her head spin. What had occurred back at the hotel? What was she about to find out? They wouldn't talk about it at lunch because they said something about police protocol and fill in their boss first.

They reached the Lieutenant's door with no response from Kelly, and Lauren found herself seated in a chair outside Jake's office as she predicted, while they moved inside without her.

"Hmmpfff!" Lauren grew impatient waiting on an explanation.

She sat there, in front of the glass window, twisting her hair between her thumb and fingers and wondered when she would ever be part of the conversation regarding herself. The vibration of another text broke her train of thought.

Hey, it's me. Don't be mad, but I snuck down here. I'm outside the police station, are you able to come see me for five minutes?

Yeah, I'm thinking they wouldn't be a fan of that, but I can certainly ask. They are in a meeting right now though.

Please, what can they do? Arrest you for talking to me?

I'll interrupt them and try.

Lauren went to the door and knocked. Gus responded immediately while Joshua seemed to be in deep conversation with Lieutenant Halverson.

"Yes…"

"Sorry to interrupt, but my friend Kelly is down stairs and wants to say hi. I'm just gonna run down---"

"Are you out of your mind?" Joshua had now joined Gus at the door. Clearly, he hadn't been nearly as engrossed in the conversation as she had thought. His eyes were wild and he had a baffled expression on her face.

I knew something happened.

"No…I'm not out of my mind at all. I'm in the perfect frame of mind for a person who doesn't have a fucking clue as to what's going on." She spat.

"You are absolutely right, Lauren. How about this, I will come with you, just to look out for you, and then we'll fill you in afterwards," Gus patted her on the back.

"Thank you, Gus." She threw daggers at Joshua as she huffed away.

"Oh! We're going now?" Gus briskly walked after her toward the elevators. The office door shut loudly behind them.

Gus and Lauren stepped outside and looked around for Kelly. There were many cars traveling up and down the street and parked at meters, as it was still afternoon in the middle of a workday. Quite a few pedestrians also littered the sidewalks in front of the station, as well as across the street, but she couldn't discern Kelly from any of the other figures on the sidewalk or in the cars.

"Huh…she said she was here." Lauren pulled out her phone. Nothing. She sent her own message.

```
I thought you were out here already, I'm
down here with an escort. Did I miss you?
```

A cool breeze seeped through her clothes and blew her hair straight up. She shivered and hugged herself for warmth. After ten minutes and no reply, Lauren contemplated asking Gus if he smoked.

"Well I guess we go back in and maybe she'll get ahold of you after a while. We can always come back down."

She shook her head, but not in disagreement with him, just confusion as to where Kelly had gone. *This is so unlike her.*

Lauren followed Gus, but became more worried when she

noticed the concern on his face. He seemed to scour the area with eagle eyes before walking back into the building. Back at the Lieutenant's office, he briefly stated that Kelly was a no show, but gave Joshua a knowing look. Joshua then shot daggers of his own at Lauren. Obviously, still unhappy with her insisted departure. *Whatever.*

She took a seat far away from him and listened as Gus and Lieutenant Halverson explained what had occurred at the hotel.

"How did he even know how to find me there?"

"He appears to have followed us, based on this note Hanson found right before we left the parking lot of the hotel. That is why we don't want you out of our sight or putting yourself in other people's line of sight." Joshua almost growled at her.

She rolled her eyes, "Fine. You're right." She paused and put a hand over her heart, before she quipped "Wow. I see what you meant before. It does hurt to admit when you're right."

"We are working on plans for a new place for protective custody. We have to take different cars, maybe duck down with different drivers maybe." He ignored her sarcastic comment.

Her phone went off in her hand again. This time it rang instead of vibrating. *A call and not a text?*

"This has got to be Kelly. Do you mind if step out?"

Joshua opened his mouth to protest but Jake distracted him this time with a wave and nodded at Lauren.

As soon as she was outside the office she answered her

phone.

"Hey! What happened to you?" annoyed Lauren huffed into the phone. Kelly didn't say anything.

"Kelly?" she paused. Before she could say anything else a voice broke the silence.

"Lots will happen to her if you don't do exactly what I tell you. And don't misunderstand me. I will do a lot of horrible things to her, but the final thing I will do is kill her," a surly male voice said into the phone.

"What!? Who is this?"

"Don't lose concentration, Laurie. And try to practice those facial expressions. Give it away to the police and she is dead. Tell them and she is dead. You have about fifteen to twenty minutes to get to the north side of this building. You'll see me in your car."

She shuddered. *How does he have my car?*

"How? What…? I – I'm gonna need more time than that."

"Look, I'm full of nice guy moves, but fifteen to twenty minutes is as much as I can give you before I need to worry that you have sicced the police on me. And if you do, Kelly is dead. Even if I get caught, she'll be dead before they get to me."

An uncomfortable silence filled the air. She no longer knew what to say. The familiar voice. The 'nice guy moves' comment. Her stalker *was* Tony. Why did she keep ignoring all of her own intuitions?

He began to chuckle softly into the phone.

"I'm guessing you've figured out who I am. Good, then you know I have access to Kelly and that I'm serious. I'll be in contact via text from now on. And I'll send you a little extra motivation. Twenty minutes. Starting now." Then the phone flashed back to her normal screen saver.

She closed her mouth, which had been hanging open. Luckily, she had moved down the hall and had not been in view of the window where the detectives could have seen her. She needed to pull it together and fast before they did see her.

She had not come up with a plan yet when her phone dinged again. A tiny paperclip appeared next to Kelly's name. *Oh no. A picture. This won't be good.*

She swallowed hard and made sure her back was to the office. She suspected whatever the photo contained, likely, it would evoke an emotion too difficult to hide. However, she couldn't have predicted how deeply she would despair.

Kelly's eyes were wild and scared. Tears streamed through black mascara, which streaked down her cheeks. Her eyes also pled with the camera. With Lauren. Perhaps they pled with anyone who might see this photo. But Kelly had to know Lauren would get this photo and therefore she truly begged Lauren more than anyone else. She had masking tape, not just on her mouth, but wrapped all the way around her head. Lauren could see it had become stuck in her long blonde hair. Kelly's face reminded Lauren of Mrs. Mason, the first day she had seen her. Bruised and beaten, but Kelly also had a split lip and a cut on her cheek.

She knew in that moment she had to risk even the smallest chance of rescue. They weren't best friends, they were sisters. She silently longed for the days when they were kids with their little girl drama of pushing each other in dog crap and not speaking for weeks on end because one of them had dropped out of the girl scouts or they had a crush on the same boy. She wished for the days before they went on those first dates.

Okay. Plan. I need a plan. I couldn't even stand outside the damn police station alone, how in the hell am I getting out of here?

The phone dinged again. It was Tony on Kelly's phone.

```
Tick tock. Tick tock.
```

Fuck!

Lauren subconsciously bit on nail. *Well maybe I tell him I need to use the bathroom and then what?* She became anxiety ridden. Lauren followed the rules from birth, so this would be a difficult feat for her in many ways. First, she would have to lie. Not a thing she was good at. She tapped a foot on the ground and then took a deep breath. Nervously, she walked back into view of the window and waved to Joshua. Second, she had to trick them and third she had to ninja her way out of this building without alerting detectives. People trained to detect.

She hadn't fully planned out her lines by the time he opened the door. She quickly slipped her phone into her purse and a gust of hot air stepped out with Joshua. He opened his mouth to speak, but she didn't let him.

"I really have to use the bathroom."

"This will only take a few more minutes; can you come back in first? You can wait a few minutes, right?" he asked holding the door ajar.

"It really can't wait. I don't think I need to give you details, but I certainly can go into the gross female specifics, if you want."

His face screwed up in disgust, which gave her a sense of pride and put a grin on her face for eliciting the reaction she had hoped for from him. In a time like this, she needed that.

"What is with the condescending tone?" This time *he* rolled his eyes at her. "Fine. Whatever. It's down the hall t…nevermind, I'll take you. It's not the same one as before. And it's probably better that I come with you anyways and look out for you. Even if you are snarkier today than you were yesterday, but at least now you have hinted as to why."

"Ugh," she complained. She lost patience with him. Time slipped away and she wanted to scream and cry. She wanted to run out of there and just get this over with. *How am I going to get away with this when Mr. Detective is underfoot?*

It hit her. She had to play on the obvious flirtation that went on between them. Her hands became clammy because she knew these things didn't play out like they did in the movies. She bit her lip as she tried to come up with a plan on the walk to the bathroom.

She needed to get his phone away from him or his handcuffs. Silently, she snorted at herself. *Right. Sure. I'll kiss him and then sneak his cuffs off him and somehow be fast enough and strong enough to maneuver his hands to a high enough level where he can't reach his phone to call for back up. And how would she stop him from yelling out? Breathe… I need a new plan, one that, hopefully, works.*

She sulked as he led her to the bathroom. She realized she couldn't simply climb out the window as they were on the second floor. However, when they entered the bathroom, she glanced toward the window to see if she could squeeze through it.

She would need to examine the bathroom to weigh all of her options, before she tried the riskiest of them all. *Is there even anything to hit him with? Do I even have the strength to knock him out?*

First things first. She took a deep breath and headed to the window in the bathroom. It seemed a little high for her, but the heating vent provided a ledge for her to step on. The window sat in between the last stall and the sink with a mirror on the wall. Her shoulders slumped down in defeat. A fall from this height would likely cause her to break both of her legs, if not her neck.

She strained to see if there was a ladder or fire escape, anything to scale. Two windows away there was a pipe of some sort, but she worked for a law office, not the circus. She could barely do a pull up as it was. Propped up on her tippy toes, she stood on the bathroom vent and her chin barely cleared above the bottom of the window ledge.

Frantically, she looked around the practically empty bathroom. No closets or cupboards. Just the basics. Not even a mop in a mop bucket that a janitor might have carelessly left behind. The type of thing they do in almost every movie. This would be no reenactment of the scene from _Annie,_ where Molly took a mop and hit Pepper in the face with it to aid in her escape. Her sure to fail plan of sex appeal and fast moving hands had to work.

Okay remove the handcuffs, handcuff him to the stall, don't get overpowered by him. Save Kelly's life and try not to get killed in the process. Simple.

She cringed. This had to be the worst of all the plans she could have ever thought of, but it was the only plan she could come up with. She had already thought of the obvious plan of telling Joshua. Maybe they would "tail" her and Tony, but she didn't think they would go for it.

Note to self, Lauren, real life, not TV. Why couldn't this be TV?

She had begun pacing in front of the only two stalls available in a bathroom with windows so small, that only Houdini could escape from it. Midstride she almost tripped when from behind her she heard a deep voice faking a cough. She didn't even want to turn around. The knowledge that her time ticked away faster than she could even keep up with it, flustered her, as did his very presence. *Has it already been fifteen minutes? How much time do I have? What the hell is he going to say? What should I say? "I'm freaking out right now." I can say that, that's not a lie. That's not a lie.* She whirled around and almost smacked him in the process.

She jumped back, startled. He had crept up right behind her. She couldn't even guess what thoughts must have rolled around in his head right now.

"Sorry," she stammered.

His expression did not betray his thoughts, but her stomach unleashed a giant field of butterflies upon her. She felt her cheeks bloom with color. She tried to convince herself it had to be the plan that made her nervous and nothing more. He took the same step toward her he had taken in the hotel, but she forced herself to stand her ground. His eyebrows raised at the same time his head cocked slightly, registering her lack of movement. Flames filled her cheeks again. Faltering, her gaze fell. She felt a large, slightly rough, but gentle hand under her chin raising her head to look at him. *This might have been a bad plan.* He held her gaze as his free arm wrapped around her waist and pulled her into him. The back of his hand swept across her red cheek before wrapping around the back of her head, weaving his fingers through her soft, brown hair. Through the haze of nerves and electricity flowing throughout her entire body she almost forgot what she needed to do.

She shook herself to her senses and placed her hands on his lower back, where she hoped to find his handcuffs. However, the moment his lips brushed hers, she forgot the plan.

BZZZZ BZZZZ BZZZZ They both jumped.

Oh thank God. I suck at this.

He didn't release his hold of her though, as he grabbed his vibrating cell phone from his back pocket and read the message that had come through. She watched his face, his expression, and waited as patiently as she could. She needed to move and yet she didn't want to move. She wanted the kiss more than ever before.

"Shit." He mumbled as he put the phone back and pulled her back impossibly close to him. Lightly, he brushed her lips against his again, before finally letting her go, slowly. The open-ended kiss drove her past the edge of sanity, but she had to get her head clear.

"They have some preliminary tests back on another case I'm working on down at the…" he trailed off. "Well they need me to come down there for a few minutes. I'm going to get another officer down here to escort you, unless you are done doing whatever it is you were doing in here," He teased before adding, "We can finish this later."

She finally regained her composure now that he wasn't so close to her, but her heart pounded so loudly in her ears, she wondered if he could hear it too.

She sighed in relief. She could forego the whole plan and

sneak out before the officer showed up.

"Uh…Fine… Yeah… I still haven't…I need more time, so that would be great. Thank you. Just tell him or her to wait *outside* of the bathroom."

He winked at her in acknowledgement and swung around toward the door. Sadness replaced her relief. *Would that be the last time she ever saw him? Would that be the last time she ever almost kissed him? Or any man for that matter?*

"Wait." She called after him. She felt breathless and her heart raced once more.

He turned toward her and looked at her expectantly. As bravely as she could, she walked over to him determinedly, and wrapped her arms around his neck, before pressing her lips to his. At first, he didn't seem to respond, but his hands were back in her hair as his lips responded to hers. His kiss gentle, yet urgent and passionate. Hungrily, they searched with their lips and tongues.

When they finally pulled apart, his eyes were still closed and his hands were now on her hips and she felt out of breath and dizzy.

"You better get going. Like you said, we'll finish this later," She smiled and let go of his neck. She knew she had to move now before she missed her chance, so she pulled away from him.

Wobbling a little, he slowly opened his eyes and sheepishly rubbed the back of his neck again.

"Yes, yes we will." His eyes sparkled a little before he

turned and left. Her heart still hung in sadness, but she no longer felt regret.

She grabbed her purse, fumbled for her phone, and looked at the time. *Thank God, I have a couple of minutes.* Lauren paused by a toilet with her phone in hand. She stretched her hand over the toilet with her phone, but pulled it back to her body. Tony hadn't said anything about her phone. She shoved it into her back pocket.

Carefully, she pulled opened the door into the hallway and poked her head out. She didn't see anyone. This initially surprised her. It appeared a more private bathroom he had brought her to. She saw an exit sign at the end of the hallway, the opposite direction she had come from. Likely, he had gone to the morgue. Once the rest of her body was out of the bathroom, she scurried as nonchalantly as she could toward the exit door. She then pushed open the heavy door to the stairwell. She turned and gave one last look to be sure no one noticed her leaving. Still, no one.

She sucked in her breath as she ran down the stairs for fear of being caught. For fear of actually making it to meet Tony and possibly being murdered. For fear of tripping on the stairs and breaking her neck. Beads of sweat had formed on her forehead. Her breath was ragged, but not from the two floors she had just flew down. Her heart raced from sheer terror. At the bottom of the stairs, in a dimly lit stairwell, she stood before the door to the outside world, or so she assumed and stopped. She took three deep breaths. *Here we go.* She pushed the door open and the gloom of the day had not dissipated since entering the station earlier. If

nothing, else, it became more overcast with dread looming over

her. She stepped out onto the sidewalk. *Goodbye, Joshua.*

CHAPTER 19

Once Joshua requested a watch at the bathroom door for Lauren, he turned the corner and leaned up against the wall. He rubbed his face and looked at his wrist for the time: 309 pm.

"Get it together, Joshua," he rested his head against the wall. He didn't want anyone to see him scold himself for his unprofessional behavior. *Why did she have to be so..?* He had only intended to peek in on her, but she looked so distraught. He learned quickly, when she paced she was upset, especially when she bit her nails, which understandably had been quite a bit since they met.

Something seemed off earlier, while he sat in the Lieutenant's office. He could have sworn she looked nervous and scared. His instincts were always on point and those instincts steered him into the bathroom.

When he had opened the door and she wasn't in the stall, he felt he had confirmed those suspicions, because she was rather, obsessively, circling the bathroom. He felt himself vindicated when he busted her. She clearly, was not in an urgent need for the bathroom as she had claimed. However, when she finally turned around and blushed again...*Oh God! What am I doing?* He pushed himself away from the wall.

Forget it...just get the lab results. Focus on the job, which I should be doing anyway. There are two cases that need to be solved. You love this job, don't fuck it up. But that kiss, that was, wow, what was that even about?

In all reality, he wasn't sure if he LOVED the job as much as thrived on it. It kept him sane after Renee had died. He knew this job better than anything and he trusted the job more than anything. If he lost this job because of breaking protocol or policy, he would lose a part of himself. Half the time he wasn't even sure he liked her, so why risk it for lust? He lowered his head and rested his back against the wall again.

He straightened himself up. Still lost in his own thoughts, he slowly trudged down to the coroner's office. The coroner had new information about Madison and Tanya, supposedly. His stride picked up as he thought about the possibility of solving that case. Giving their families the answers they needed and catching their killer.

At the end of the hallway, he pushed open the door to the

morgue and wandered back to the brightly lit office. He had never fully adjusted to the smell of death, but it no longer made him queasy. He passed a few other employees who had just rolled a body back into one of the labeled drawers. This is where they would stay until after a completed autopsy or until the family came to claim them.

"Hey Linda, what do you have for me?" he asked the fifty something coroner as he stood next to her. Slender, with grey-blond hair tied up in a loose bun, she also wore glasses around her neck and a white lab coat.

She smiled, "Hey there handsome. I only have a little bit for you. It was hard to really get a lot off the bodies because of the water damage as you know, but from what I can gather, they both were raped multiple times, due to bruising and lacerations that I found. Madison was stabbed 17 times and Tanya 18 times before he sliced open their throats."

"So, we have a clear head wound that Madison sustained from other injuries prior to the actual murder? I guess I hoped for a little more earth shattering news here.

"Well, Madison seemed to get the worst of it, but like I said, most of the evidence washed away, so DNA is out of the question," she flipped through a manila folder, lifting pages as she spoke.

"Anything else?" Defeat painted his expression.

"Okay, the blood on the locket belonged to Tanya. Dead

end there. If you can find anything else, we can see if we can get a DNA match in our system or CODIS."

He shoulders slumped, "So we are going to have run an M.O. search and see if we can find anything similar. Thank you so much Linda for your help. Let me know if anything else turns up."

"Well I thought you might be interested that time of death indicates that Tanya died first. I'm no detective, but I found it interesting, if Tanya was the girlfriend, that he murdered her first. Could be nothing though."

"That is interesting. Again, let me know if you find anything else."

"Get me a DNA sample and I will." She winked at him and put the file back on her desk.

Disappointed with the little bit of information she passed onto him, Joshua's step went back to a slow trudge.

Gus rushed into the morgue, panicked.

"Let's go! She's gone!"

Huh? What- Fuck! I knew it, I knew she was up to something. Gus had sweat on his brow and seemed out of breath. Joshua threw an odd look at him.

"I was looking all over for her and running." Gus defended himself winded, but when Joshua raised an eyebrow at him, he just added. "Forget it. I'm fat."

Gus ran back out and Joshua followed his lead back to the bathroom where he had last seen Lauren. *Lauren's gone? Where in the hell would she go? She can't be this stupid!?*

"What the hell's going on?" They stood outside the bathroom with Officer Moore, who had stood guard.

"Well, Officer Moore waited here for a few minutes. He finally gave a knock when she seemed to take too long, and when no one answered, he went in to check it out. She was already gone before he even got here. She moved quick, or she was taken quick," Gus sputtered still breathing heavily. "It doesn't appear she went out the window, 'cause that would be impressive. I think the best way out would have been that exit down there."

Joshua lost in thought, replayed everything, but from a different perspective than the first time. Her sudden need for the bathroom, and no longer being irritated with him. She didn't pull away from him when he finally went in for the kiss. He had hoped his charm had finally won her over. He shook his head and combed through the bathroom himself to check for any other clues. He did notice something on the window. A layer of dust on the air conditioner had two clean spots, shoe sized. He peered at the ledge of the window and could see finger marks in the dust and dirt. She had been looking for a way out, it would seem. She wasn't forcibly removed. He couldn't be a hundred percent positive, but he hoped that to be the case. *That's what the kiss was all about.* He fumed with embarrassment at his foolishness. He turned to Officer Moore and Gus with a look of disgust.

"She left on her own," he said stone faced.

He couldn't even be sure the footprints and fingerprints were from her, but he made a safe bet based on the size of the impressions in the dust.

"First things first, let's see what we can find out about our killer and in the meantime, Moore, track her phone's GPS location." Moore wrote down the information, nodded, and rushed away.

"Second, I'll try and get in touch with Kelly. She was supposed to meet her earlier and never showed, right? Let's see what's up there."

Back at his desk, Joshua disconnected the call with Kelly's voice mail after leaving her a message. She didn't answer. From what he could tell, the woman always had her phone glued to her hand. Hopefully, once she heard who left the message she would call back and quickly.

He flipped through his notes from the first night he met Lauren; he had yet to even file the report, and he poured over it for any clues. Every so often he would peek up and look for Gus. Upon his last look, Officer Moore handed something to the ADA, hopefully the subpoena for the text messages, but Gus was right; it would take too long and he knew they had to move faster. He scoffed as he realized the notes contained nothing of any value to their search.

He focused his attention on his computer. He wasn't going

to stop for anything, and logged into facebook. *If I have to go door to door I will*. He felt helpless. He pulled up Lauren's name. He reviewed four different pages until he finally landed on the correct Lauren. He grumbled when he discovered most aspects than not of her account were private. He regretfully wished she had been a little less wise, a little more naïve, and used less restrictions on her page. He clicked on "photos". Before he even looked at the first picture available for viewing, Gus snapped his fingers from his desk to get his attention.

He got up without looking at the screen and stood by him until Gus hung up the phone. He wrote furiously on a scrap of paper.

"What is it!?" Joshua asked impatiently.

"Lauren never picked up her car from work."

"Yeah…" he said with some annoyance. Joshua didn't think there was anything to gain from the car or contents.

"So…if she didn't pick it up, where did it go? I just talked to her boss, Beth. I'm gonna put an APB for her car and see what we turn up."

Joshua patted Gus on the back. "Let's see what else we can find. Hopefully, we'll get a call on the car sooner than us needing anything else." He did pause to wonder how this guy could have been sloppy enough to take her car. He got up and went back to his computer to examine the few pictures. He grabbed his cup of coffee. The later it got the quieter the station became. There were only a few people left in the office. He took a sip and glanced at his screen. Lauren and Kelly, he assumed. He scrolled down to the 2nd and 3rd pictures. More pictures of the two besties. The boyfriend, Tony, sprung to mind, but it came as no surprise to Joshua that Lauren didn't have any pictures of him. She made it clear about her feelings toward the guy.

He continued down past the fourth photo, fifth, and…. Joshua stopped and went back up. Just like all the other pictures he had viewed, this picture contained a smiley Kelly and Lauren, but something caught his eye around Kelly's neck. *These have to be all over the place, right?*

With hands shaking, he reached into his drawer and pulled out the Madison and Tanya file. Slowly he opened it, and held his breath. He flipped through crime scene photos, one after another, until he found the object of his search. The treasure he had found at the cabin, the silver locket with just the picture of Tanya in it. He stared at it. He double clicked on the picture of Kelly and Lauren and blew it up as big as he could and held the hard copy photo of the other necklace up for comparison.

They were identical. Only one thing would solidify it, the inscription on the back. He needed to get ahold of Kelly, quickly, unless it was already too late. Perhaps that's why he hadn't heard back from her. His mouth gaped open and he perspired. After everything the coroner had disclosed about Madison and Tanya, he instantly felt sick to his stomach about what might become of

Lauren. And he feared what had already become of Kelly.

Okay think. Madison and Kelly died around the same time, so maybe he just snagged Kelly. Maybe the girls are together.

Lauren took off to save her friend from a crazy boyfriend. She would have no idea what she walked into or what this guy was capable of. He stood up, ran his shaky hand through his hair. The helpless feeling only increased further. He had no idea where to even begin to look for them. His emotional attachment caused him to draw a blank.

From across the room, Gus must have noticed his visible panic. This time Gus came over to *his* desk before Joshua could even look up. In the few moments it took for him to examine the contents of Joshua's desk and the images on his monitor, he came to the same conclusion. Joshua watched the color drain from Gus' face.

CHAPTER 20

She headed in the direction Tony had mapped out to her while her eyes scanned the streets for her car. It became easy to blend into the busy afternoon, but she feared that she looked suspicious. She nervously looked over her shoulder, afraid that at any moment Joshua would catch her. She had no idea what waited for her. And he had her car. She stopped in her tracks when she saw a familiar car a block away from her. The familiar sleek black, newer four-door vehicle threw her off. She knew he took it, but it still jarred her to realize her own vehicle would aid her capture. The shadowy figure waited in the driver seat and Lauren could make out Tony's shape. The fact she knew the stalker didn't make it less haunting. She rubbed her arms briskly as a chill spread up her spine, even with her coat on.

She moved again, when she could tell he gazed in her general vicinity. He had seen her. Overwhelmed with sadness and fear, she recognized she hadn't fully committed to this act. She could still turn around and run. Deep down, she wanted Joshua to find her just in the nick of time.

With each step, she advanced toward him, she knew it would not play out that way. She hugged herself tight to quiet the foreboding tremors that ran through her body. Lauren reached her own vehicle to the sound of the door unlocking loudly. An arm reached out from inside and signaled toward the back seat. Reluctantly, she moved toward the passenger, backseat door and opened it. She crawled in, setting her purse on the floor of the car.

"Having fun yet, Lauren?"

"Is Kelly all right?"

"You answer my question first, that's the rules." He spoke firmly.

"I guess I didn't realize this was a game, Tony. No, I'm not having fun, but that's the answer you want, isn't it?" She leaned back in her seat and folded her arms in front of her chest. *I really need to check my attitude; this guy could potentially kill me. Lose the attitude. Think smart, Lauren.*

As he pulled away, he spoke softly, "It's only polite Lauren, basic kindergarten rules, right?" His voice became more loud,

"Now buckle up! I don't need the game to be ended so quickly over something as stupid as a seatbelt."

See, now you pissed him off, damn you, Lauren.

Upon examination of Tony, Lauren furrowed her brow in confusion. Even though he yelled, his expression fell neutral. That same weird calm expression he wore the other two times she had interacted with him at the restaurant and at Kelly's home.

She fidgeted in the passenger seat of the car. His presence in her own vehicle removed ownership from her. The car now belonged to him. It smelled of his cologne. It overwhelmed her nostrils and silently, she gagged. She recognized it from the restaurant and she hated it even more than she did then. *Why would he be wearing cologne now?* The only thought that came to mind she couldn't bear to continue to think about. It instantly brought on a queasy sensation in her belly.

She couldn't get out even if she wanted to, and he likely utilized the handy child safety lock feature. However, she wouldn't even attempt it. She wanted to be here to ensure the safety of her best friend, if she could. Alternatively, and quite foolishly, she may just have made sure Kelly had a partner in death. This had to be the dumbest thing she had ever done, she concluded.

At that moment, it dawned on her he hadn't answered her question, so once again, she asked, "Is Kelly okay?"

His expression didn't change, he continued to drive. Was he not going to answer her? But when he finally did, she wished he hadn't.

"You really need to start worrying about yourself."

The haunting words sank in, but she couldn't help her response because it was honest.

"If I did that, I wouldn't be here. I'm here because I'm worried about her."

Finally, a new expression. He seemed to be mulling over her answer as if he had never heard it before, but she very much doubted that. He just nodded and added, "She's fine for right now."

For the next hour, they sat in silence. She had almost fallen asleep at one point, but the first time she locked eyes with his dead looking ones, she worked hard to stay awake. His eyes were black, cold, and lifeless.

They exited onto a deserted ramp off the freeway. *Are we almost there? Are we almost to Kelly?*

He turned down the frontage road. From the freeway, this road remained hidden by tall pine trees and fat bushes. He slowed down a few feet past a big pro-life billboard and stopped. When they pulled directly behind a parked, gold, four-door sedan. Lauren's eyes went wide. The car from her office, the black hoodie in Kelly's closet. The rest of her body fell paralyzed in shock, until she heard his laughter. *But of course, why would it be anyone else?*

"Recognize it?" He practically slithered.

"Of course, it was you." She dropped her head down.

"Oh man," he said excitedly as he turned to face her. "You were so close to seeing my car, that day, in the garage. I thought my heart would explode. I can't remember the last time I felt fear.

You gave me quite the rush."

Oh my God. What is he going to do to me? Blood-thirsty lust poured from his eyes. Her heart raced and her hands grew clammy and sweaty.

"Oh, calm down. I wish you could see your face. I got you good. Probably thought you were going crazy," he snickered, as he reached into the front passenger seat. He lifted a black object up in the air for her to see. *Is that the hoodie. What a sick bastard?*

He dropped it with another giggle, got out of the car, and went to the trunk. He continuously inspected his surroundings. He removed some items from her car and proceeded to his car. He did this several times and checked, for what she could only guess were oncoming cars, until he had finished all the necessary transfers. He appeared to have saved her for last. The sun was already starting to set at 430 and shadows crawled forth from the bushes and the road.

She wondered if she would go in the trunk or if she would be left here, dead. Second to Tony, the anticipation might just kill her. She waited nervously and gasped when he headed toward her side of the car. She regarded her own car as a traitor, the thing that helped him transport her to some awful fate. She realized if she lived through all of this, the car would be the first thing to go.

He opened the door, and ripped her purse out of her arms and jutted his hand out to signal her cooperation. Robotically, she exited the backseat, but did not take his hand. His cheek and eye twitched in response to her defiant act and he roughly grabbed her by the elbow, pinching her in the process. She winced at how tightly he gripped her. He continued to yank on her, still looking around cautiously. He opened the door to his car and angrily pushed her into the seat. However, once again, when she looked up at him, he had no emotion. It was just a flicker across his face and then nothing. Her stomach tightened when she comprehended what kind of person Tony might be. She knew this would be dangerous, but nausea hit her when she worried that she might be dealing with a sociopath. Filled with dread, she could only cling to optimism. *I'm just being paranoid. Tony is a garden-variety domestic abuser. Nothing scarier than that. Please, nothing scarier than that.*

Every cop show about serial killers tried to flood and drown her positive thoughts. Every TV psychologist she remembered speaking on sociopathic behavior, popped into her head. They always mentioned the lack of emotion and empathy. She witnessed this first hand from Tony. Though she was no expert, she had looked into the eyes of a soulless creature for the first time in her life.

So much for positive thinking.

He leaned over her to grab her seatbelt and startled her. *Is he going to strangle me with it?* She closed her eyes tightly until she heard him chuckle again. Her eyes popped open in confusion and terror. His laugh, a sickly sneer, if a sneer dared to be audible. He paused and stared at her. She swore she saw desire on his face again. *Get there faster, Lauren. He wants your fear. Don't give it to him!* After a few more awkward seconds, he continued to snap the seatbelt into its lock. Without warning, his hands ran up the length of the strap, which crossed over her chest and very deliberately ran an open hand across both her breasts, before he stroked her cheek.

She turned her head in revulsion and shuddered at his touch. It contrasted, starkly, the moments whenever Joshua got too close to her. Butterflies fluttered and sent a sensation of tingles throughout her body. Not this moment. This moment had an equally strong affect, but caused nausea, not giddiness. Her stomach turned and rolled until she felt the vomit rise. The color drained from her face. This sensation wasn't just obvious to her, her captor saw it too. Tony pulled back and for the first time, she saw an emotion: anger. Her fear amplified as he raised his hand. When it came back down, her cheek stung from the slap he issued, hard, across her face.

The crack of it echoed across the deserted road and back into the car. Her eyes welled up with tears, but she turned away from him and bit her lip to quiet herself. She didn't want him to have satisfaction or her pain. Her fear stimulated him, and with her latest rejection, he upped the ante to get that stimulation. It's what he wanted from her, or at least she assumed.

"It doesn't much matter what you want anyway. I just assumed someone who throws herself all over some "has been" cop or a complete stranger in college, however many strangers that might be, wouldn't really say no to anyone." He pressed his lips up to her right ear and whispered fiercely, "But...it doesn't much matter, does it?"

How does he...Why does he...how long has he been watching me? He had to be watching me long enough to never lose track of me in the first place? Or is there another way he is keeping tabs on me?

"Now do yourself a favor, don't fucking move." He rocked the car as he slammed it shut and headed back to her car after picking her purse back up off the ground and threw it into the trunk. She wondered if he noticed her phone wasn't in it. She knew she played with fire, but he never asked for it so she intended to feign ignorance.

Finally, in the driver's seat, he turned over the engine and slowly turned the car back toward the freeway to continue their journey. However, Lauren had no idea where that journey would end. As they passed her car, she realized the plates weren't even hers. He must have done it before picking her up and she never noticed. Therefore, even if Joshua knew her car had gone missing, they wouldn't find her. And if they did find her, it wouldn't be in time.

She broke the silence that had been going on ever since they left her car behind, "Can I ask you why you are doing this?"

She figured a sociopath wouldn't have a reason she could understand, but she felt compelled to open a dialogue.

"Does it really matter. The whys? Do you want me to tell

you I was abused as a boy, or my mommy didn't love me, or I simply like the game? What are you hoping to gain from this line of questioning, Laurie?"

"Satisfying my curiosity, maybe. So, this is a game to you? Why Kelly? What made you choose her?"

Once again, he released a laugh that left her cold. She obviously missed the mark on his motivation. *What did I miss?* She felt her body tense up as she braced herself for the reality of his true motive.

She raised a hand to bite a nail.

Crack. Tony slapped her hand away.

"Don't do that." He squinted his eyes at her.

What the flying hell!?

"You stopped smoking, you can work on this nasty habit now."

Her head spun from the change up. *How did he know I used to smoke? Did Kelly tell him all of this? So, what could this be about?* She thought back to how all of this had started. He didn't really seem keen on meeting her, but yet, based on the things he knew, he had been watching her for some time. Everything focused on her from the start. *Why not try to date me instead?* She rubbed her red hand and stared forward with a creased brow, trying to figure out the illogical. He briefly glanced at her. He seemed to enjoy himself as he watched her try to figure it out.

I would never find him attractive. Too uptight. Why am I

trying to figure out this crazy person, there is no logical reason for this?

"You really think this is about Kelly? Man. I try to pick smart women. Makes the game more exciting, but all you smarties always seem to be oblivious to the most obvious part of the game. Madison thought it was about Tanya too. Sarah thought it was about Jessica, and they (neither of them) were very smart."

Madison and Tanya? Why does that sound familiar? She couldn't remember, but she knew when he listed the names it only confirmed her previous suspicions about him. Her shoulders sunk with her heart. Part of her held to the idea, that maybe, just maybe, they could get out of this.

"It's about me for some reason, but I'm not going to bother…." She trailed off as she remembered that night a few weeks ago, sitting in her living room. She had turned the channel because she couldn't watch anymore or hear any worse news…

'…"…AND AFTER ALMOST A TWO-MONTH SEARCH, THE BODIES OF 28 YEAR-OLD TANYA BURK AND 29 YEAR-OLD MADISON TALBERT HAVE BEEN RECOVERED. WHILE THEY HAVE NO SUSPECTS IN CUSTODY, IT DOES APPEAR THAT THEY BOTH DIED FROM MULTIPLE STAB WOUNDS. AN AUTOPSY HAS BEEN ORDERED, BUT THE FINAL RESULTS OF THAT WON'T BE AVAILABLE FOR A FEW MORE WEEKS. THE POLICE DO HAVE A PERSON OF INTEREST. GAVIN…"…'

The newscaster's voice filled her head, repeating it over and over.

"You're Gavin…. And Tanya and Madison are…are. *You killed them*," she trembled. *Was this the game? He plays it out to this point and then kills us both?*

"She wasn't the one." The sarcasm poured from his lips.

"So, you were after Madison, and not Tanya, but why?" Lauren decided to approach him from a different angle and take the focus off herself.

"I wanted her, but I knew she would never have me. She thought she was better than me. Always did. Always suspicious of me. Like you were and still are. I knew it from that first time we met. That bitchy comment at the bar. Your stiff reaction to my hug. You tried to cover it up, just like she did. She wasn't as good at it as you are. Bitch thought she could get away from me too. Had to teach her a lesson. Can't say I don't love giving lessons. So, as much as I'm hoping you don't make me teach you something tonight, there is a bigger part of me that wants you to." He never looked at her just stared ahead as dusk drew upon them with a creepy smile on his lips. She couldn't let it end there, she had to bring him out of this trance.

She took a deep breath and finally asked the direct question, "Why us?"

"Ahhh…yes. I was actually leaving town. After Madison and Tanya, the smart thing would have been to leave, but as I packed my car…did you know Tanya lived two houses away from that party you went to? Anyway, I saw you and Kelly, well I saw you. You went into that party. It was so packed with people, I knew no one would notice. I just pretended I knew someone inside and the moron answering the door let me right in. No questions asked. And then I watched you and waited."

A slithery tingle ran up her spine.

"What are you going to do to us? What do you wa---"

"I think we are done sharing," he cut her off. "It won't be all bad, you'll probably like some of it. You seem like that type of girl," He turned on the radio and raised his index fingers to his lips which curled and dribbled with sadism and madness.

Lauren's face twisted in disgusted bewilderment. Quite possibly these psychopathic rantings were not grounded in any reality, but she sensed something more behind the strange insult. Tony took immense pleasure in her reactions. *This damn face of mine that instantly reveals all my thoughts.*

He smiled as he looked over at her momentarily. Then he turned his attention back to the road and dialed the music back down.

"I'm almost disappointed that you don't remember that night. You seemed to enjoy parts of it. I know I did, Laurie," he said sensually, while he patted her on the thigh.

She cringed at the nickname. She thought maybe she misheard him the first time, but there it was again. Then the touch made it worse. *Do not flinch. Do not flinch. Try not to gag.* She regained her composure.

"What night?" although she knew what night. They weren't nightmares. Tony's mouth opened and all her ability to deny what might have happened was torn away as soon as he spoke. She felt sick to her stomach. She silently prayed it was just more insults, like those regarding her intelligence. Perhaps, just another way to get under her skin and tear down her self-confidence.

"I'll tell you this much, I am not disappointed with what I was able to see and touch that night. I wanted a whole lot more, believe me, but Kelly's lights wouldn't go out. She must have a higher tolerance than you to the drugs I slipped you two."

She had a sudden and intense desire to shower, cry, and throw up. He *had* touched her. His hands had been all over her. She could only take solace in the fact that it didn't sound as if more than that occurred. One small break. *Thank you, Kelly, for your ability to hold your liquor or whatever.*

She sank in her seat. Before she could get any words out he turned the radio back up. She knew well enough not to say anything more, not yet. She didn't want to hear anymore anyway. She wanted to get the hell out of the car.

Kelly crossed her mind and she wondered whether he had already killed her. She had no proof of her still being alive. She was exhausted from all the things that were happening around her, but she didn't want to risk falling asleep. Her eyes felt heavy now that the hairs on the back of her neck had finally gone down. She knew while he drove, she had a little more time. She urged them open, but tried not to make a sound. She didn't want to draw his attention to her, but the quieter she became, the more sleep pulled at her. Her body finally succumbed and her eyes shut completely, closing out the nightmare that had come to life.

She jerked awake, her arms thrashed out to protect herself from some kind of attack. Tony had grabbed her by the legs and proceeded to drag her out of the car. She scuffed her hands as she tried to use them to protect her head from the ground. Steam poured from his ears as he said things she couldn't make out. He mumbled instead of shouted. Now wide awake, the dark and cold November air hit her body as the heels of her shoes hit the ground when he finally released her into the ditch.

"What!? What's going on! What are you doing!?" she screamed and pleaded at the same time, but it fell on deaf angry ears. He pushed her back to the ground and forced her face first into the earth. He straddled her at the knees. She tried to see around her, but besides the brown grass all around her and pine trees that ran alongside the freeway, she wasn't positive what road they were on the side of.

He grabbed her by her hair and leaned down pressing his mouth to her ear.

"Did you think I wouldn't find out, bitch!?" he breathed

heavily, still seething. Crushed under his weight, she couldn't catch her breath. His hand pressed into her head, and smashed her cheek into the ground. She coughed as she tried to take in air when she felt his free hand roaming all over her body.

Oh God, he is going to rape me.

"Wha..what..what did I do," she sputtered and tried to distract him. She could hear the cars whiz by in the distance. He said nothing more, until his hand found the bottom of her sweatshirt and pulled it up.

"NOO please!" she screamed and squirmed fiercely.

"Shut up!" his hand rested on the back of her jeans and she knew instantly what he was truly after. She felt relief for a second before she recognized she could be in far more danger because of his discovery.

He reached in and grabbed the cell phone from the back pocket. Out of the corner of her eye, in the awkward position she was in, she could see him briefly scroll through it. He let out a snort.

"So, I guess it doesn't matter anymore," he spoke coldly. She put her hands up to her head instinctively to protect it and waited for something horrible. He sat silent for some time and she felt him stare at the back of her head, as if he tried to burn a hole into her skull and read her thoughts. Before he slammed her phone into to the ground, smashing it into pieces, he put his hand on her back.

"It doesn't matter anymore because we aren't meeting Kelly. She's dead. I learned my lesson the last time. One at a time is much more satisfying. Madison. Pffft…she almost screwed up the whole plan."

He got up, but just enough to force her over to her back. She could finally breathe again and for a moment, she noticed the clear deep blue night sky and all the brilliant stars in the night sky. She also realized the temperature had dropped quite a bit. Her teeth chattered quietly, and she could see her breath in front of her. The information slowly sunk in and yet she couldn't find the tears. The fear overwhelmed any other emotion and the sudden motivation for escape. Even if he killed her in the process, she no longer had a reason to not try and get away, unless, she thought, he planned to kill her right here.

Though he straddled her waist, she didn't want to look at him. Too afraid to look him in the eyes and see whatever he might be thinking, she tried to avoid eye contact. Then she finally made herself turn her head toward him, as she shivered on the cold ground. Her hands were free, but she lay frozen, motionless.

She wondered how much time had passed as he sat there just staring at her. She watched his breath curl around him like prophetic smoke. She hoped that rage inspired him to hurt her with lies of Kelly's death.

What did he see on my phone?

He finally spoke again, but now he smiled.

"I don't know what it is about you Laurie, but I just can't stay mad at you. I know that I didn't tell you that you couldn't have your phone. And since I did kill your best friend, we'll call it even.

He's absolutely crazy.

The smooth charmer returned in his voice. She almost missed the rage. She had gotten used to that guy, but this new guy who said horrible things with cold, calm poise scared her more. Then, to hear him talk sweet, in an almost comical way freaked her out more than any other version of him. The precarious situation they were in, physically, became obvious to her, and she needed to come up with a plan in case he hadn't already discovered that himself. She had a hard time finding the words and she felt her face begin to regain the color since it had previously drained away. The bitter wind nipped and felt like tiny shards of glass pelting her cheek, probably from the small cuts from the ground she had been smashed into.

"I..I'm sorry, I didn't think about it…umm..I have to go to the bathroom," she stammered.

He scanned over her body with his eyes and leaned close to her face, "Hmmm…there's plen…" headlights cut him off and drew dangerously near to them. The sound of slightly squeaky breaks and an engine coming to an idle after the transmission shifted gears.

He hopped up and looked toward the noise of the vehicle.

He quickly reached for her arm to pull her up, but swiped at air as she took the opportunity. She could feel her heart exploding in her ears and her labored breathing deafened her. She panicked at the thought of how she would know if he gained on her and if her recapture was imminent with all the noise echoing in her head. The hard ground crunched under her feet and she ran wildly in no particular direction. She wanted to run to the safety of the car that had pulled up and distracted Tony, however, he stood between her and the car. They were close enough to be heard, but not seen. She ran in the opposite direction toward the woods and just kept running.

For a brief moment, thoughts of Kelly sprung up. She quickly pushed those thoughts down. *If you survive this, you can grieve then.*

CHAPTER 21

How could he let her slip through his grasp? He sat in front of Jakes's desk and floated in and out of the conversation while Gus updated the Lieutenant. He would go back and forth between worry and fear to anger and annoyance. He couldn't believe she could be so stupid and not involve him. *What the hell was she thinking? Who does that!?* Joshua talked himself down and realized, it sounded like something *he* would do for someone he loved. Lauren loved Kelly and she risked her life, most likely for Kelly's life. They had a car out to Kelly's place, they had people working on Lauren's text messages, and tracing the GPS of her phone. But it didn't feel fast enough.

Jake's phone rang on his desk. When he finally hung up he faced his detectives.

"We got some news." Joshua still lost in his thought stared right through Jake.

"King!" Jake waved his hand in his face to get his attention. Joshua sat up and looked at his boss, and then Jake continued. "We did find some similar unsolved cases in other states. Two girls and a mysterious boyfriend, but this looks like the first case where he could be hitting the same state twice. Lauren and Kelly could be the second set of Minnesota women. The first ones were in Texas, and they were fortunate enough to get DNA. They didn't find a match in CODIS, but we have something to compare and link the killer to. That is if we catch him, and if it truly is the same guy, we'll know pretty quick."

"So, he is devolving or escalating," Gus thought aloud.

"Maybe, or maybe he just couldn't resist Lauren for some reason," Joshua said and got to his feet. There was no time to travel to these other states and conduct interviews with the family members of those other victims, but perhaps he could reach someone by phone who worked those cases. Ultimately, he knew the fastest way to Lauren was the GPS, but until that information found its way to him, he collected everything he could so he would know the best way to handle Tony, Gavin, whatever his name was, when he finally ran into him.

They may not have an exact name, but they at least knew who this person was to Lauren. Like with Madison, it was her best friend's boyfriend. Joshua knew they were in Madison's family cabin and it appeared the other crime scenes took place in rural homes belonging to one of the two girls. *Is that where he's headed? Some family cabin that Kelly or Lauren owned?*

"Where is my location!?" he stuck his head out of his boss' office and yelled into the main room.

More commotion began outside Halverson's office as Moore leaned over his computer with the analyst assigned to the GPS.

"Just a few more seconds….Got it! We can't get you the exact location, but we can tell you where it's pinging off the closest tower. So, you'll be within a few miles at least." Moore tore the piece of paper from the notepad that the location was written on.

Joshua immediately swiped it from his hand as he pushed past him, quickly heading toward his desk. He grabbed his coat and keys as Gus tried to catch up with him.

"What are you going to do, partner?" Gus questioned as he stood in front of him.

"This gets me closer than connecting with the other cases. Just make sure they are still feeding me updates on anything they discover. Find out if she or Kelly have a cabin in the area and we can then figure out the most logical paths from there. Patrol can go up and down those roads, maybe roadblocks to check the vehicles, but I HAVE to be out there. I can't sit here anymore."

Gus nodded his head in understanding, but remained on his

heels. Joshua knew Gus had no intention of staying behind. Before they hit the double doors leading out of the station, their Lieutenant and another officer stepped in front of them. They both wore solemn expressions. Joshua's heart stopped and he searched Halverson's face for a clue.

"Jones just got a call from dispatch. The long and short of it, it appears that they found Kelly Masters' body. From what they can tell so far, she was badly beaten and raped. They found her in her basement under a pile of clothes. The coroner is on her way to determine exact time and cause of death." Lieutenant Halverson patted his shoulder before he added, "There was no sign of Lauren." Detective King's lips tightened and his resolve intensified. He felt instant relief she didn't suffer the same fate as Kelly, but then the worry of a fate worse than that of Kelly's sprung to mind.

"But that is veering from his M.O. if it's the same guy. That's all the more reason I have to go. He's becoming unpredictable in his pattern. Keep me updated on everything. Gus will fill you in on what we are looking for," he faded out down the hall, but Gus still tailed close behind him. He shouted back to the Lieutenant, as well.

"I'll call you with those details in the car. I'm with him."

Joshua wasn't going to pause to argue with him, he just needed to find her. He couldn't shake the fear he felt. He rocked between the hope that he wasn't too late to find Lauren and grief that if he did find her, he would need to deliver terrible news of her friend's death.

Mostly, he had no idea what direction to go in. All he could do was drive toward the area of the tower and hope more leads would call in from the station. Perhaps this Gavin or Tony person would get sloppy due to an inflated sense of ego and invincibility, he thought wistfully. With Lauren and Kelly, he had grown ballsy, but Joshua hadn't figured out why, yet. Again, maybe more information would shed light on some of this. What drove Tony to so quickly to seek out another girl or girls? And to come to the police station? But, of course, they didn't know what he looked like.

They were following the trail with the help of the police that were working the other murders. Now that they believed that these cases were tied together they could help each other.

"Hey, can you clue me in on what's going on in there?" Gus pointed at Joshua's head, once they were in the car.

"Well I'm sure you are thinking the same thing I'm thinking. Why so soon, why so ballsy, why these two? He seemed to have too much information on Lauren. He paid too much attention to her, even though he dated her friend. We missed something. We missed the biggest piece, we are missing his motivation. It had to be about Lauren the whole time. He just threw Kelly away." He mumbled the last sentence as he thought to himself. Gus piped in and spoke over Joshua.

"I agree, Madison and Tanya, it wasn't as clear cut. Do you believe that he meant to go after Madison the whole time and not Tanya? Or do you think she just got in the way? And how does this help us figure out what his next move is, besides hurting Lauren? So far that seems to be his only motive or ambition." He stopped short of stating the obvious, that likely Tony would try to kill Lauren, as he had all the others. Though Joshua noticed, he ignored the absence of the words. He also knew Gus did it for his benefit. Renee's death had changed him. Gus had to know the loss of another woman in Joshua's life, could potentially break his spirit.

Gus' phone went off before Joshua could even think of a reply, let alone register the information.

"Yeah? Really? Okay. Thanks. We're on our way" He hung up on the caller and turned back to Joshua who was shaking his head.

"Stop with the headshake, a cop in Pine City found Lauren's car. Not her plates, but the VIN number matches. It was found abandoned and completely empty," he emphasized the empty part for Joshua's benefit, "It's sitting on a frontage road off 35 North. So, we are headed in the right direction. They will tow the car to the station for a more thorough forensic search after we had a chance to examine the car ourselves."

Joshua squeezed the steering wheel and accelerated by another ten miles an hour. *I have to save her.*

CHAPTER 22

Her heart pounded in her chest as she ran. Lauren tripped and almost lost her footing, but she caught herself mid-stumble. Though she wanted to cry or even give up under the overwhelming pressure and fear, she knew she couldn't. She pushed through two large pine trees and lumbered into an opening where she found herself in a parkway or street. It appeared to be a town home complex under construction. She approached from the dead-end side of a clump of houses. Several of them looked to be completed from the outside and as she stepped out into the cul de sac, she could see further down the road. There were several buildings in the beginning stages of construction. Out in the open, her skin bristled under the cooler temperature that the evening had become since she had first climbed into the car with Tony. The sweat on her head and face chilled her each time the wind hit her. She also became aware she stood vulnerable due to her visibility to passersby.

Unsure of how closely he might have followed, she backed up quickly when she heard a car coming down the street and lights flickered ahead near the entrance. With the car moving slowly in between the new homes, she knew she had time to hide. *It has to be Tony. He doesn't know exactly where I am, he's searching. He must have gone back to the car instead of chasing me. What became of my "good Samaritan"? Did they drive off unaware of my predicament?*

She fell back from the direction she had emerged and stayed behind the closest house, one of the completed homes. She got ready to run back to the road, but she grew cold and tired. She peeked around the corner and saw the hideous gold car as it drew near. *Fuck it!* She spun on her heels and ran towards the tree line she had come from before Tony caught a glimpse of her. She was two steps from the edge of the woods when her foot snagged on a tree root hidden from her in the dark. Lauren landed hard, but her hands caught her fall first.

"Dammit, that was dumb," she whispered. She pushed herself up to stand and fell back to the earth. She slapped her hand over her mouth as she almost screamed out in pain. A tear rolled down her cheek from the stabbing pain from what she could only guess was a twisted ankle. She continued to sob softly as she realized the danger that she was now in had become heightened by her injury.

She reassessed her surroundings and hopped to the back of the house, poking her head around the corner. The car sat in the middle of the street, running idle, and there was no sign of the driver. The headlights were still on and pointed in her direction, blinding her from distinguishing any shapes inside the car.

As quickly as she could, she hobbled over to the next house, which hadn't been completed. She heard plastic move quietly from the light breeze that blew against it. The plastic sheet covered a huge gaping hole that protected the unfinished home from the elements and any wildlife. Carefully, she pulled at it and peered inside. She found herself in what she imagined would eventually be the main level of this home. Houses further down the street were still wide open, with just the beginning stages of development evident and they offered no true shelter. With all her might, she forcibly pulled at the plastic and made a big enough gap to squeeze the rest of her body through. Her plan was to leave little to no trace of her presence, should Tony come back this way. Frantically, she searched around the room, hoping to find a staple gun lying on the floor so she could cover her tracks, but no such luck.

A responsible construction crew, awesome.

She tugged at her ear as she took in her surroundings. She appeared to be in a possible living room and realized the "gaping hole" was likely going to be a sliding door eventually. Something that led to a nice patio and perhaps a nice view of something in the summer. It was hard to envision in the dark, and in all the heart pounding terror of what this night had become.

She moved toward the stairs at the opposite end of the room. This floor contained no rooms, no completed closets, nooks or crannies, or hiding places of any kind. Only wooden two by fours and studs. *Too easy to find. Maybe I could wait til he comes through the back and hope ...* "what, Lauren? Wait til he leaves the keys in the car too? Right in front of the house?" She whispered to herself. "Yeah, right."

She tried to listen for him because she didn't want to get too close to windows and risk being seen. There were no concealing curtains, but her heart still pounded in her ears and she couldn't hear a thing between that and her labored breathing. She needed to calm down and get control of her herself.

"Who am I kidding?" She shakily whispered.

With no ability to hear well, she inched herself closer and closer to the window to try to peek out. Her ankle began to throb.

Her eyes fell on the split entry staircase. Quietly, as she could manage, she limped to the stairs and decided to inspect the basement in hopes of finding a good place to take cover.

When she reached the bottom of the stairs, she found the first window that pointed towards his car and the cul de sac. Curiosity pulled her forward and she went to look. She strained and grunted, as she had to be on her tiptoes to see out. She saw shadows pass in front of the headlights and she thought her heart might explode from the terror that pumped through it. She dropped to one heel.

Her breath faintly created a fog on the windowpane. She held her breath and hoped he hadn't seen her glimpse out the window.

Bravely, she inched once more, back up on her toes toward the window. She had to know. She peeked through the steamy window to get a better look. Her eyes darted towards his car. Her breath whooshed out of her. She wiped the window that fogged up so much, she could no longer see through it. The window, now cleared, revealed a man in uniform. A policeman! She dropped back down to her one good foot and took one excited hop toward the stairs before she stopped again. *Why would a cop be driving Tony's car?*

She went back to the window and pushed up onto her toes one last time. The varnish of the windowsill seemed stronger with her nose practically planted against it. The "cop" now drug something across the front lawn of the house she currently hid herself in. *He's coming in here!?* Lauren dropped down again and winced from the pain but looked for any exit. She couldn't get out of any the high windows, even if she hadn't been injured. *No egress windows? Really? Of all the damn luck!?*

She heard glass shatter up above her and a few moments

later loud footsteps clumped around and echoed off the bare walls and uncarpeted floors.

She found the furnace that hadn't had walls built around it yet, and crammed her body behind it, hoping the darkness would aid her in hiding should he come down.

He has to know I'm here. There is no other explanation. Or he is one damn lucky bastard.

He fumbled around upstairs for quite some time, never saying anything. If he did know she was there, he did not attempt to communicate with her. *What the hell is he even doing up there?* She came out from behind the furnace and sat next to it. The pulsing of her foot became too much for her to stand on. Then she heard him at the top of the stairs, so she braced herself, ready to hide quickly and quietly behind the furnace again. It sounded like he dragged something heavy *up* the stairs. *Thank God.*

She shivered in the cold basement and huddled near the furnace that unfortunately had not been turned on yet.

Clomping footsteps came back down the stairs from the upper level. Her body tensed. Then she heard the front door slam shut.

She got up as swiftly as her ankle would allow, and went to the window. She watched, who she was confident was Tony, get back into his car and drive it down to the end of the street before throwing it in park once more.

What is he doing now? The window pane squeaked as she

wiped it of her breath again.

Tony, slowly got out of his vehicle, and walked towards the first house. *He doesn't know where I am.*

Then he disappeared into that home and with as much speed as her injured foot abled her to, she limped up the stairs and to the front door. Her cold fingers wrapped around the even colder door handle. She dropped her hand when she saw him reappear, smoke seemed to pour out of his ears and steam literally rose off his body. He crossed the street to the next house.

Now's my chance, I have to go back the way I came. He is going to search house by house until he finds me.

She remembered the gaping hole in the back of the house and turned towards it. Her mouth dropped open. In front of her only exit out were heavy looking wooden planks that would take too much time in her state to move. There had to be twenty of them. It had to be the entire pile she barely registered when she passed them. If she remembered correctly, they had been stacked in what would likely be the kitchen someday.

Her heartbeat felt like it came to a complete stop for half a second and she slowly peered outside once more. She pulled the handle while never taking her eyes off the last house she saw him go into, and took one slow step. *Thump!*

A scream that escaped her throat came to a grunting halt when she hit the ground with a thud. *What the hell?* Steps she assumed would be there, were not. Not yet, anyway. Though she only fell a foot, it still hurt. She hadn't even had time to put out her hands to block her fall. She shook when a new thought struck her. She had screamed. He had to hear that in the dead quiet of this neighborhood. She pushed herself up, and still resting on her hip, she frantically scanned the street

Shit! She flailed, floundered, and forced herself up and back up the huge step into the house. Tony stood directly in front of the door of the house that she so carefully had watched. He didn't move, he just seemed to glare at her. As she fell inside the house in a state of panic, she felt grateful for the adrenaline that pumped through her body. It would delay the pain that she surely would be feeling later.

I'm a smart woman. Why can I not come up with an escape plan? She dealt with women before who tried to evade a dangerous ex, she thought she might have learned a thing or two. Though in her defense, she had never seen someone deal with a serial killer before. She sucked in her breath and took a quick look out the window of the now locked door. However, she knew there were two ways into this house. The broken window in the front and he could push his way through the back as he was likely much stronger than she.

Her heart galloped away, and she wanted to scream. Tony closed the distance between them unhurriedly. Clearly, he didn't worry that she would escape, so weakly, she pulled herself up the stairs. *Gotta hide.*

CHAPTER 23

The minutes ticked by on the drive up to her abandoned car. Located forty miles outside of the twin cities, northbound, they were only a few miles from the targeted exit when Gus' phone rang.

"Gus Harris here."

"Really? Any bodies? Anything at the scene? Cell phone? Don't move anything, we'll be right up." He ended the call and put it back in his coat pocket.

"Skip the exit, we have to drive a little further to another scene, likely it's related."

"Are you sure it's related?" Joshua gritted his teeth in agitation. Not wanting to take the chance on going elsewhere and wasting precious moments with a killer who seemed to be making many mistakes and escalating.

"I'm pretty sure, Joshua. From the description, they found her cell phone not far from the car."

"He stole another car?"

"No, it appears that a local uniform pulled over to a car running on the side of the road. This officer, Officer Hendricks, is now missing, but his car's still there," before Joshua could interrupt with the obvious comments, Gus put up his hand and continued quickly.

"Where the car is sitting is in the location that he called about." Gus shook his head.

"Is he dead!?" Joshua asked.

"They don't know, there's some blood near the vehicle and drag marks. But there is no sign of Lauren, Hendricks, or our suspect, but they are getting the dogs out there to see. It's hard to say right now."

"I guess I can't act surprised that he would kill a police officer, but yet I am. I'm more worried that the police will be gunning for him and Lauren could get caught in the crossfire. How much further up the road is this scene?" his grip on the wheel had become slippery from sweat.

"It's about another hour down the road. Drive as fast as you can, man."

They pulled up forty-five minutes later next to a brilliant array of lights on squad cars, flashlights, and camera lights from forensics. The sky glowed with an ominous flashing red and the trees nearby cast ghastly shadows across the frosted earth, which stretched and shrank with each blink of the strobe lights from the police cars. Joshua shivered. The crimson glow threatened their evening with menace and unleashed sunset at high speeds they weren't prepared for.

Parked off to the side of the road sat what he could only assume was Hendricks car. Overrun with forensic specialists and many different departmental officers, the vehicle had become a new crime scene. Cameras flashed and yellow caution tape adorned the grounds around the car and disappeared in the dark, near the edge of the trees. The squad car marked the outer edge of this tapeline. Joshua's eyes went immediately to yellow triangle shaped markers in the earth that indicated evidence. It was about twenty yards from the car. His stomach swirled and he felt a level of fear he hadn't felt since Renee had first disappeared, before they found her body buried in some forest. Dread welled up inside him for a woman he barely knew.

He was a wreck, but it motivated him at the same time. He hoped all of this only meant that they were catching up and not too late. Moreover, he hoped they would catch up in time to find her in the same shape he'd left her. After what happened to Kelly, he wasn't even deluding himself that Tony's plan was anything less.

He got out of the car and passed by the lead detective on the scene as he nodded at Gus for him to handle those details, including his own identity. He went straight to the little yellow markers strewn all over in a circle and, apparently, upon closer inspection, a trail leading right into the woods. The dogs must have picked up a scent, maybe they even found footprints.

He squatted down by the markers, where a struggle must have ensued based on the drag marks and the flattened grass that he now hunched over. He guessed this is where they found her phone as well. He grabbed a small flashlight from his breast pocket and once again went over the earth, just in case he saw something the crime scene unit didn't see. He stood up and followed the rest of the trail markers. *Maybe she ran through here or someone did.*

He signaled to Gus.

"Can you stay here? I'm gonna check this path out, see if she went that way, but in case they didn't, you know in case they both got back in the car together, you'll be here to follow that lead if it comes in?"

"Of course. Just take a walkie." An officer, he didn't recognize responded to Gus' wave and handed him a walkie talkie from the local police. "Just in case."

He patted Gus on the back of the arm and continued to follow what appeared to be an easy foot trail. Something she might have taken if she had a chance to run off. He'd give it a little bit and if he found nothing he could come back.

He pushed forward, shoving his coat back to expose his holster and cautiously placed his hand on the butt of his 45 as he entered the wooded area. He should have asked how deep the forest extended, but he just kept walking instead.

He imagined the steps Lauren might have taken, and tried to feel how she felt. *Does she know her best friend is dead? Is she already dead herself or injured?* He searched around calmly to see what she might have seen, but decided she likely (out of fear and through possible tears) took the path of least resistance, and headed that way himself.

Though it was far enough where the homes couldn't be seen through the trees, it didn't take long before the woods gave way to a backyard to a cul de sac of townhomes still in development. He could hear plastic flapping in the distance. The wind blew between two units and sent a chill up his spine. The houses he faced were practically finished in construction. It was only a matter of time before homeowners would begin moving in, maybe even weeks away. He slowly walked toward the sound of the plastic and tried to take in his surroundings. Listening to every sound...

Lauren awkwardly climbed the stairs looking behind her

most of the time. As she neared the top she looked down for the last time and then she heard the front door open. She gasped and took the last step up as Tony stepped through the entrance.

She rounded the corner of the landing and walked directly into some obstruction hanging from the ceiling. Her mouth fell open and she could feel the color leave her face. She froze in shock.

A man's body. She suddenly comprehended what Tony had lugged through the front yard. She remembered she had thought he was a police officer when she saw him through the basement window because he wore a uniform. Could this be the body of the owner of that uniform? She was face to face with him, strung up by his feet, throat slit, and a pool of blood beneath him on the floor. His fingertips dipped in the pool and his eyes were wide open, flat, and lifeless, but they told the story of the terror he experienced in his last few moments of life. The wound in his neck frowned at her, with red blood like drool still dripping down over the sides of his chin and head.

She dizzily looked down, followed the trail of the sinister fluid, and gasped, the tips of her boots were now coated with it. She clutched her stomach and wavered unsteadily on her feet. She couldn't stand and she couldn't stop her fall, which caused her hands to splash in his blood. She fell further forward into the cool, wet liquid.

Move! Move! Move! She screamed in her head. Panicked

anew, she quickly tried to put her feet underneath her again and stand up. Each step a struggle. In all the horror, she hadn't heard Tony come up behind her, just felt a hand in her hair and the same sick overpowering smell of his cologne. He pulled her back into him. She felt the wind and hope knocked out of her as she hit him and she cried out from the pain in her ankle.

Lauren reached out to keep her balance, and accidentally grabbed the officer's body. She yelled out when she felt his body under her touch and the wet stickiness of his blood smeared onto his white t-shirt.

She cried quietly. But as she stared at her bloody hand prints she left behind on the poor cop, she began to convulse. Tony released her and she fell to her knees again, and began to retch and gag.

Fluid pour from her mouth and nose, while he chuckled. When she finished, he lunged down and pulled her back up. Then pushed her toward the back of the room toward a load-bearing stud. As they reached the beam, they stood near a window and she glimpsed the shape of a person down below. In that small moment, she saw a man with brown hair. A man with a gun. *Please let it be him.*

She released a high pitched, blood-curdling scream and immediately she fell painfully to the ground when Tony shoved her down and kicked her in the stomach. She curled up in a ball and cried. Lauren could only hope he didn't see Joshua as she had. She begged him to stop when she thought he was about to do it again. He did, but not because she asked him to.

She never noticed the walkie until it burst to life with a staticky chatter. On the other end, a voice she recognized. Joshua. Tony's face twisted up with rage and the short-lived truce ended when he kicked her again.

Joshua carefully walked behind the houses and listened for a struggle, footsteps, or even God forbid screams from Lauren. One foot slowly in front of another, he reached the other side of the house. He checked behind him once more before coming up to the next house, weapon drawn, ready for Tony to be there. Waiting.

Halfway through the next backyard, he heard a chilling scream coming from up above him. He grabbed his walkie in one hand, while propelling his feet forward and holding his gun firmly in his freehand.

"10-96, officer in need of back up. I have a possible 10-67 at a town home complex under construction. This is Detective King. Gus!" He reported into his walkie.

His walkie crackled with static and it screamed back at him into the silence of the night air. He dropped back as an unfamiliar voice came across.

"Hello Detective King, you must be close, but are you on time?"

He stood quietly as he realized their missing police officer must be missing his walkie too. *Dammit.*

"Tony is it? Can I talk to Lauren, just to be sure she's okay."

He waited with fearful anticipation.

"Joshua. I'm okay," but she coughed and wheezed.

"Hi Lauren. I'm glad to hear your voice. Are you upstairs in one of these houses?" Joshua replied. He held his breath hoping to hear her voice again.

Silence. Crackle. Silence. Crackle. Silence. The silence ticked by slowly for Joshua.

Crackle.

"Come on, I think we all know where we are at this point. I guess the question is, will you get to her before I'm done with her. Now, if our brave little girl here doesn't try to be brave again…bah…" Silence. Then Tony sighed deeply into the walkie and something rubbed against it, like his cheeks or his mouth perhaps. Crackle.

"Who are we kidding, Joshua, I have no intention of letting this woman live. She has disappointed me so much in the last few hours." His voice became rage filled as the sentence ended.

"I spent so much time on her. Watching her, following her, sending her special notes, and even some very special presents and look at the thanks I get."

The detective could feel his hands getting sweaty and his

heart rate increase. He believed Tony when he said he wasn't going to let Lauren live. However, another thought had occurred to him. *Did he value his own life though? Would this guy expect to escape alive or did he simply not care?*

His walkie crackled as he depressed the button on the side. He slowly raised it to his mouth and leaned back against the side of the house.

"Yeah why kid ourselves?" He did his own deep sigh and hoped Tony was crazy enough to buy the change of attitude. They, after all, hadn't spoken before.

"I mean if it's a competition for Lauren, you can have her. I'll let you both go, alive. Is there anything I can get you?" He smacked his head into his hand. *I'm not a damn negotiator.* He clicked on the button again and signed, "I think you and her could leave here with no one getting hurt."

He released the button and held his breath as he waited, for what seemed like an eternity for a reply.

Crackle...

"Well, I'll say this for you detective, you really are trying to make this work. I appreciate that. Or should I say, you are really trying to work this."

CHAPTER 24

As Tony and Joshua proceed to have a conversation over walkie talkie that likely the entire police department could hear, Tony pulled her sore and wounded body up and cuffed her hands behind her around the beam, forcing her to a seated position. She felt a pain in her ribs she had never experienced before. *I wonder if this is what a broken rib feels like.*

She tried to aid Joshua's efforts.

"Yeah Tony, neither one of us has to die. We can get out of here, maybe you can even drop me somewhere and you can just go. I won't---

"Shut up, Laurie, you are on the verge of begging and that doesn't suit you," he raised a hand up in annoyance and she flinched.

Her reaction to this motion caught his attention. Soft laughter emerged from Tony and his eyes gleamed. She wondered why either she or Joshua wasted their breath. Tony may have wanted to live, but he had no desire for her to. He took way too much pleasure in her suffering and she knew it.

Crackle…

"Okay, you got me. I'm not a negotiator." Silence. "Tony? What can I offer you? Perhaps we can do an exchange of some kind. Me for Lauren? You know, to help you get out of here with a bigger piece of collateral?"

Tony studied Lauren's reaction to Joshua's words and in typical fashion her emotions registered on her face, and then so did his. Her eyes widened at the thought of either one of them being in his grasp. Even if she would have gone along with the plan, she couldn't disguise that the idea distressed her.

"Pffttt," Tony said with disgust and then picked up the walkie again.

"Typical woman. Puts out all of the signs and gets cold feet and pretends she doesn't want you when you decide to take her up on her offer. Like the first night Lauren and I met. Did you know she was into me, Joshua. Flirted like some whore. Her best friend's boyfriend and she could not control herself. Then she lied to Kelly and said she wasn't. Lied to me and said she wasn't." As he waited for Joshua to reply, he winked at her.

Silence. No response from Joshua, no words uttered from

Lauren.

His words twisted in her. He truly believed the crap he fed Kelly. Disbelief struck her. He kept staring at her intensely. *Now what? What is he looking for?* She just turned her head slightly away and blinked back tears. They were genuine, but they were from fear not from sadness. Is that what he wanted to see? He seemed to be satisfied at her new state of worry and defeat and turned his attention back to Joshua.

The conversation continued back and forth while she looked around the room for anything that would help her concoct a plan or help her to escape. Maybe something Joshua could use in a rescue. She noticed it had grown quiet as her neck craned behind her inspecting the room. She swallowed hard before facing Tony who simply stared at her. A combination of anger and bewilderment painted his expression. He seemed to see right through her and know her thoughts. That's when she saw the knife in his hand. She didn't even remember seeing it before, but clearly, he had one if he killed the police officer earlier in the night. He had to know what she had been thinking. It couldn't have been that big of a leap, but what sparked that look? He seemed fine one minute and now...

Something had changed in his whole demeanor. He didn't seem human anymore.

"Why do you insist on pissing me off, Laurie?" he hissed. "You know," he moved closer to her, "I saw you at that party. You know the one where I met Kelly, and I knew I had to have you. Can't say I'm not mad that I might miss out on that opportunity…or will I?"

"What do you mean?" Her chin popped up and she had to consciously force it down to avoid further retribution.

He closed the distance between them. He brushed her hair with his fingers while Joshua tried to get his attention.

Crackle

"Tony, are you still there?"

He finally rolled his eyes, pulled the walkie between them, and pressed it to his mouth.

"You are interrupting me, man, it's so rude. Hold please."

Crackle…

"So, where was I? See, I saw you earlier tonight, sneak behind this house and not come out. I think you were so busy trying not to be seen, that you didn't realize I went behind the house looking for you. Figured out pretty quick how you got in. Shit, figured out pretty quick that you went in at all. I knew the whole time you were in here. And, if Detective Party Pooper hadn't shown up, this would have been a very fun and long night."

He rubbed a thumb down her cheek and over her lips. She tried to turn away as she squeezed her eyes shut, but he grasped her jaw in his hand and forced her to face him.

"Lots of thoughts about what I was gonna … what we were gonna do in this house," he gritted his teeth. His anger rising again at her reaction.

He picked up the walkie again.

"So Joshua. Dee -TecTive King," Tony mocked, "Has your back up arrived or did you find a way to signal them without using the radios?"

Silence. He glared at her and didn't take his eyes off her. He stayed within inches of her. So close, she could feel his breath on her. It smelled bitter and sour. She tried to bite back the gagging. In her mind, the evil inside him ate away at him until he rotted.

Crackle…

"No, it's still just us. They don't really have an exact location of where I am, as you could hear. I'd like to come on in. Talk man to man, face to face. Maybe we can work out a deal. What do you think?"

Silence.

Tony shifted from sitting to a crouched position, still burning holes into her head with his eyes. She wanted to back up or away, but she pressed into a beam. There was nowhere for her to go.

Crackle... He raised the walkie.

"It's been fun having this conversation, but no. This is mine to do with as I please, but believe me when I tell you this, if I hear you come in I will kill her instantly."

Silence.

Crackle.

"Tony, let's talk about this,"

Crackle.

Silence.

He tossed the walkie over his shoulder.

"Good bye, Joshua."

CHAPTER 25

"FUCK!" Joshua yelled out after Tony had ended the transmission. Lauren's time drew to an end, and he knew it.

He continued around to the front of the house, listening intently for any further sounds from Lauren. The grass, covered in leaves and twigs, had grown cold from the November weather. They snapped and crunched under his feet.

He knew this had to be the one. The house where the screams had come from. He gazed at the broken window by the front door and his eyes fell on the jagged pieces jutting this way and that. Joshua found more glass inside the doorway as he approached. He backed up and paused. He raised his head and looked up. No one peered in any of the windows. Joshua shivered with gun still drawn as he glanced around him. The front door felt too obvious. He cautiously pursued his original path toward the big door. He grabbed the handle and held his breath as he pressed down on the lever. Locked. He gently released the cold metal and his breath. He stepped off to the side of the window and peered through before reaching in and gently unlocking the door.

The plain grey siding seemed to make the drabness and dreariness of the evening even more gray and daunting. A twig snapped behind him and he whirled around. He breathed a sigh of relief when he saw Gus and a couple of other officers work their way around the house the same way he had. He stepped backwards and signaled them silently by raising one hand like a stop sign and the other hand he held to his lips.

Gus approached his partner with weapon drawn and whispered, "You should go around back and enter through that plastic. There's an opening right there, but wait until we break down the door, loudly. Maybe this gives us a little bit of an edge? We might be able to get the jump on him if he thinks you are coming through the front instead of the back."

"I agree we should go through both entrances, but the back is actually blocked by beams and two by fours. Your men push that shit over and make a ton of noise and then you and I go through the front. Most likely he is expecting that we'll come through both anyway." Joshua said firmly.

Gus just nodded and went around back to relay the plan to the waiting officers. When Gus returned, they waited patiently for the loud clattering.

CRASH!!!!

Tony rose on his knees to tower over her the best he could. Oddly with a gentle touch, he ran his fingers through her hair.

She whimpered, but tried not to recoil from his touch as she remembered how this had angered him before. She knew this would be a different outcome. Trapped like a wild animal, she worried he would also react like one. Though her body stiffened she tried to relax to his touch without retching.

He smirked.

"It's too bad we don't have more time, Lauren. The things I wanted to do to you before this, but now you've ruined it of course. Only enough time to enjoy a little fun." He placed a finger over her lips, expecting her to say something.

"Well, fun for me anyway. This won't be any fun for you."

He moved the blade toward her body. She squeezed her eyes shut and waited for something to happen. Her eyes flew open when a loud crash sounded from down below.

"Well, this is it, sweetie, I was counting on them not listening to my very simple directions," he wore a smug expression on his face, unsettling her. *What is he up to now?*

"Oh, by the way," he leaned toward her, and forced a kiss on her lips after he had kneeled back down. At the same time, he jutted his hand out between them. Immense pressure emanated from her side as he pushed the knife into her. Her eyes went wide again, this time in shock. Sharp pain hit her senses. Lauren became dizzy when she spotted the knife sticking out from her stomach and blood covering her shirt in a rapidly expanding pattern. Her blood and excruciating anguish washed over her.

"Can you hold that for me?" His sickening smile stretched like the Joker's as her pain intensified and she realized how helpless she was with her arms cuffed behind her back.

He patted her on the head and before he turned away, he almost giggled as he spoke, "I hope to return soon. Finish this properly. But if not, and somehow by some miracle, you make it out of here alive, I'll find you."

He pulled the dead cop's gun out of the back of his jeans, and headed down the stairs, deliberately, and oddly confident.

She could do nothing more than lean back and wait for him to kill her or slowly die from the wound he had already inflicted upon her.

Joshua and Gus waited until they could hear footsteps coming from up above. Gus instructed the other officers not to enter, just to knock items over so they still had the element of surprise from the front. When they heard Tony hit the bottom of the stairs, they burst into the house with guns drawn.

"Freeze! Police. Tony Anderson drop your weapons and put your hands on your head!" Joshua shouted at Tony's back. The officers in the back began to push through into the house, blocking any exit Tony might have had.

He slowly raised his hands into the air and dropped his gun on the floor. Gus still pointed his weapon at Tony, while Joshua came up behind him and cuffed his hands behind his back. Flashlights lit up the room with glowy stripes and struck Tony's face, highlighting a creepy grin on his face. Joshua stopped a shudder as he took a closer look at him. Now cuffed, he got close to him and just continued to examine him in shock, until words finally spilled forth.

"You! You're that asshole gardener at Lauren's."

Tony looked passed him, expression unchanged.

"Get him the fuck out of my face," he spat in disgust as he shoved him toward Gus.

"I got him. I'll put him in a squad."

He just nodded as he ran upstairs to find Lauren. As he reached the landing his heart fell into the pit of his stomach when he saw all the blood.

"Gus! Where's that ambulance!?" he shouted over his shoulder. "Lauren, hold on, someone is coming." He grabbed her wrist and felt a faint pulse. Though he sighed in relief, once more he shouted down to his partner in terror.

"Gus!!!" His voice cracked.

After Tony had left her there bleeding to death, it didn't take long before Lauren heard shouting from down below. It sounded like several voices yelling. *Freeze? Is that what they said?* She shivered and her breaths became labored and shallow.

Her eyes closed. She could hear footsteps coming towards her and her heart wanted to race, but wasn't strong enough anymore. She tried to open her eyes, but couldn't. The voice closed in on her and she felt someone touching her. She wanted to kick and flail and fight this person off but she didn't have the strength. The last thing she heard was someone saying her name, but the cold and darkness swallowed her.

CHAPTER 26

Lauren continued to run blind in the darkness. In the distance, she could see the illumination of a tiny light. Her legs weakly pumped as hard as they could as she tried to reach. The closer she got, the slower she ran and the light appeared to move away from her. She feared what lay ahead when she made out a figure in front of the soft glow. Still, she persisted and the figure took a recognizable shape.

"Kelly?" Kelly stood too far away to hear Lauren, but her own voice seemed to surprise her. She felt the weight of a hand fall on her shoulder.

She screamed, but this time no sound came out. She ran toward her best friend.

"KELLY!" Her voiced returned as she screamed for her friend whose arms where outstretched toward her. She could make out Kelly's face now as she reached for her arms. Kelly's bruised and bloodied face halted Lauren, and she tripped and stumbled. Lauren shuffled hesitantly toward her and noticed more blood dripping from her hospital gown. It seeped out from the source and formed a larger and larger circle of blood. A brilliance of vivid red enveloped the white cotton gown.

"What happened to you?" she reached for her, but her fingers swiped at air. She repeatedly tried to touch her and repeatedly she retrieved only air. She let her arms fall to her sides in defeat. She felt tears roll down her face. Her consciousness had caught up to her subconscious. She knew she dreamt and the reality was that a psychotic killer had murdered her childhood friend, her sister. It all flooded back to her. Kelly changed shape before she disappeared from her dream.

"Kelly! No! Please don't go! Please! Kelly!" Once more she reached out in vain. She just wanted to hug her one last time, and the tears wouldn't stop as she fell to her knees in the dream.

The hand dropped from her shoulder and gripped her hand. She jerked her arm away quickly, looking down for the culprit but instantly a bright light absorbed the blackness she had been in. Her eyes stung and no matter how tightly she tried to keep her eyes shut, the light still climbed through. Carefully, she tried to open her eyes. She felt cold and she noticed a funny taste in her mouth.

The brilliant light seeped through her closed lids, which still felt heavy. Lauren felt a warmth squeezing her hand, like the one in her dream. It gripped hers more tightly, but gently at the same time. She lifted her free arm to shield her eyes, but grimaced as she felt a horrible sharp pain in her side. More memories rushed in as quickly as the light had. Tony. He had stabbed her. *I'm not dead?*

"Do you need some more morphine? Don't speak. Just nod." His voice sounded distorted, but she recognized Joshua's voice immediately. She nodded. She squeezed his hand in return and sighed with relief. She must be in the hospital. She felt cold IV cords on her arms, and could hear the beep of the monitors in the room.

"How are you feeling? Again, just don't speak if you can't, just give me hand gestures. Friendly ones, please."

She smirked and tried not to laugh because she knew it would cause more pain.

She shook her head slowly, "No, I'm fine to talk." Though it did come out rough and garbled at first.

The light finally stopped hurting her eyes and she looked at him for the first time in a few days. She had missed his face and she smiled briefly.

"What happened to Tony? I didn't hear any gunshots. I can only assume he isn't dead. Did he get away?"

Joshua shushed her and tried to soothe her. "Don't worry

about it right now."

"Quit!" she rolled her eyes in exasperation. "I was kidnapped, stabbed, told my best friend was murdered, I get that you are worried or whatever, but I'm asking because I want to know." She felt worn out from the little speech.

"He's in custody. He is going to prison for a long time. Your testimony will ensure that. If you are willing to testify."

"So, no wounds of any kind?"

"Do you really want to hear all of this stuff? Don't you just want to heal and we can talk about it later?"

"No, please tell me."

"It felt like he turned himself in. He gave up pretty easily. I would be bothered by it if we didn't have him in custody with no weapons."

Her heart monitor gave her fear away. He lowered his head when he heard the increased beeping.

"I'm sorry, I wanted to know. It's not your fault I'm upset by it. He led me to believe that he would still find a way to get to me and I'm worried that he isn't or wasn't wrong. What if he does find a way?"

"I know. I'll give you this much. Texas has the death penalty. We thought we would give them the first chomp at him. He's being extradited today. We'll go from there.

"Doesn't that stuff take a long time. Years even for the trial, let alone for them to actually carry out the sentence of death?"

"Try not to worry so much." He rubbed her arm.

"It's easier not to worry when you are here." She began to feel sleepy. Too much exerting herself already.

He feigned a look of shock and grabbed his chest.

"Was that a compliment!?"

"No, I'm on lots of pain medications and very tired right now. I wouldn't take it as a compliment in this particular case," then she winked.

It was his turn to roll his eyes at her.

"So, what is the prognosis with me? I'm assuming I'll live, but what's the damage?" She asked him.

"You'll definitely need rest to help the healing process. There was a lot of blood loss, but we got that taken care of too. You will likely be out of work for some time…"

Lauren cut him off, "I think I'm looking for a new field of law anyway. This nightmare just kicked my ass in gear. I can't deal with the emotional drama and ..." She bit her lip as she chose her words carefully, "…and I think it turned me into a cynic about romance and I don't want to feel like that anymore."

She inwardly groaned. The heat from her cheeks rose and Lauren knew she blazed a cherry color. She refused to make eye contact with Joshua.

His hand brushed at her cheek once more and gently nudged her chin toward him. She finally looked up when she could feel his breath on her face. Once more, she felt his lips brush against hers.

Lauren's stomach swirled and her head followed suit. She briefly wondered it wasn't just the morphine, but disappointment filled her eyes when the kiss ended more quickly than she wanted.

"There will be plenty of time…"

BZZZZ BBBZZZZZ BBBZZZZZ

His phone vibrated in his pocket, he hung up on the call and sat down next her bed.

BBBZZZZZ BBBZZZZZ BZZZZZ

He turned his eyes to his phone to see who it was once more and once again he sent the call to voice mail. He turned his attention back to Lauren, who smirked at him.

"I don't know that much about your job that well, but I have a feeling you are going to have to take that."

"Nah, they will take a …."

BBBZZZZ BBBZZZZ BBBZZZZZ

"….hint," he pointlessly finished his thought. "Okay, I will be right back?" He winked at her and squeezed her hand before heading out of her room to take the call.

She turned her attention to the room and finally took in her surroundings, but also realized the quiet gave her time to reflect on the loss of her friend and immense sadness swept over her. Her nightmares came back to her and she wept silently. Tears rolled down her face.

She looked back toward the sliding glass door and glimpsed

Joshua as he headed slowly down the hall away from the room. She felt a sigh of relief, as she didn't want him to see her cry for some reason.

She felt weak and helpless. She relaxed further when another needed distraction rescued her just in time. A male nurse had come into the room to tend to her.

"Hi! How are you feeling today? Any better?" He asked cheerily.

"I'm as well as can be expected I guess," She wiped the tears that blurred her vision away from her cheeks.

"Good. Good. I'm just gonna check your IVs here and I'll be out of your hair so you can get some sleep and heal up," he seemed hesitant as he rounded the bed to get to the machines and the IV bags.

"I'm just gonna close these blinds too so I can dim the lights for you, if you would like?"

He was average height, blonde and seemed attractive, except he was wearing a surgical mask. *That's weird.* He seemed friendly enough, and she smiled to herself as he approached because she noticed little bits of toilet paper on his neck where he must have cut himself shaving.

She simply nodded in response. After he closed the blinds and the door, he softly whistled as he fiddled with the two bags of liquids attached to her. She had no idea what medicine they contained and hadn't asked at this point. He turned to the machine and examined the numbers like she had seen every other nurse do before.

She turned away from him to close her eyes. As they shut, she recognized his cologne, but then her eyes flew back open, wide and blinking furiously. A heavy hand fell over her mouth hard. Lauren raised her own hands to pry his off her. She felt suffocated by the weight and another smell overpowered her senses, bitter and strong. One last attempt to get him off her only pulled his mask down. She had a moment to glimpse at the face of the male nurse before her eyes closed and she could no longer control her arms as they slid back down by her sides, like game night. *Tony?*

Before she sank into darkness, she felt his lips on her forehead and then he whispered, "I just wanted you to know that we aren't done playing. I'll see you later, Laurie. Get some rest. You're gonna need it."

About the Author

Karen is from and lives in Minnesota with her wonderful fiancé, her beautiful daughter, and their fish named Dory.

When she isn't devoting time to spend with her young daughter, she occupies herself with working full time, writing, and socializing with family and friends.

She loves Law & Order, arts and crafts, date nights, and girls' trips "up North."

ACKNOWLEDGEMENTS

I want to recognize and thank the many people who have assisted me with this first book in one way or another. My friends that gave me oodles of support and some that even read parts of it for me and gave me feedback.

I want to thank my fiancé, Kevin, for reading the entire book and helping me find errors. And, for putting up with my crazy moods when I went into perfectionist mode.

I want to thank my editor at Owl Editing, Tiffany, for her critique that was constructive and yet motivational. As well as my book cover artist.

I want to thank my entire family for being supportive and being my cheerleaders for this project. I hope it is something that you will all be proud of.

There are so many more people I want to thank, but that's what more books are for, right?